THE SUNDAY RIDER

By Sally Reid

Sally Reid

Copyright 2013
All rights reserved

Sally Reid is a retired high school English teacher living in northern New York State in the foothills of the Adirondack Mountains with her husband of 42 years. This is her third novel and the third in a series about four supportive friends.

Also by Sally Reid:

The Freedom Fence
(Sarah's Story)

Arts and Graft
(Anna's Story)

PROLOGUE

At precisely 5:05 on Friday afternoon, Harvey Glavin poured a cup of hot tea that had been made by Mrs. Phipps before she left for the day, into a chipped mug, and added four spoons of sugar and a generous amount of milk. He returned the milk bottle to the refrigerator, but left the rest of the mess he made for the housekeeper to clean on Monday, and carried his drink down the hall toward his study. He dropped it to the floor when he heard a crash from the direction of the kitchen and saw walking toward him someone from his distant past. The visitor wore a knitted cap which covered his hair completely, and so it took Harvey a few seconds to realize just who that person was. "What are you doing here?" he asked calmly.

"That's not a very friendly greeting, although not quite as bad as the last time I was here."

"I reserve friendly greetings for people who have rung the front door bell and have been welcomed into my home, not for people who destroy my property and intrude upon my privacy. And this is not the first time you have done that, is it? I asked what you are doing here."

"You haven't been taking very good care of the place. All I had to do was push a bit with my shoulder against the back door and the lock came away with the door jam."

"What do you want?"

"I want you to go into the study and take a seat behind that grand desk you're so proud of so we can have a chat."

"And if I don't want to do that? If I want to walk out the door and drive away to report this intrusion to the garda?"

"I am not going to let you do that."

"Then you have a list of offences that includes breaking and entering, destruction of property, trespass, and unlawful imprisonment. This chat we are about to have must be very important to you."

"Important enough for me to travel a long way to get here and to help you along if you don't go there right now on your own."

The Sunday Rider

Harvey turned and walked toward the study down the hall with his visitor following him. He opened the door, went to his desk and sat in his well-worn seat. His visitor picked up a straight-backed chair from beside a lamp table and placed it so he could sit facing Harvey. "Well? Are you going to tell me what this is about?"

"I will in good time. As I said earlier, you have really let this house go. Have you run out of all the money that you inherited?"

"It is certainly none of your concern but it might surprise you, as it did me, how expensive these old houses are to maintain. Unlike some other great homes, this property has no inherent income. There is no orchard, or vineyard, or acreage planted in cash crops. There are, however, huge maintenance bills. To replace the roof on this house I had to sell over one hundred acres. And, of course, the heating bills are massive because the windows and doors all let in the weather."

"So you just kept selling off parcels of land."

"I did that until there was no more land to sell except for what surrounds the house and the entrances to it."

"I noticed that some of the outbuildings haven't fared very well. There seems to be one just lying on the ground."

"Yes. Several of them were in bad condition when I inherited, and I didn't want to spend what money I did have building up barns that I really didn't need. I received no large dowry from my late wife's family, as I would have if I had shopped around for a wife of more substance and class. People warned me, but I didn't listen."

His visitor bristled as Harvey spit out those words. "You're a bastard."

"I've been called much worse. Anyway, I had to make decisions. The breeding barn was in good shape and though a pair of horses was the most I would ever need, I saved that one and use it now for my one remaining horse and for storing my trailer and lawn maintenance vehicles. It's a large building, but as I said, it's in good condition. Great care was taken in its construction. I'm one person living alone and I don't need more than the one building. But none of that is of concern to you, either."

Harvey's visitor leaned forward and smiled. "I have to admit something to you. Last Sunday when you were on your ride, I came in and looked around a bit. I have even spent several nights here. You didn't know that did you? There are rooms in this house that are completely empty of anything of value. There are places where the wall-paper is falling down, the ceilings are crumbling, the lights and plumbing are off in two of the three wings. Have you been selling the art and furniture as well?"

"I sold one of the carpets in an unused bedroom for enough money to heat this place for an entire winter. And why not?"

"I'm surprised you didn't sell this gigantic desk of yours. I'm sure you could have gotten a good deal of money for it."

"This is more of a symbol than a desk really," Harvey said, rubbing his fingers across the glossy surface. "It has been in the family for generations."

"A symbol of what? Opulence, importance, prestige? How can that be when it sits in the middle of a run-down relic of a house like this? Did it ever occur to you to sell the place whole and get yourself a cottage somewhere?"

"I beg your pardon. I am not a cottage person. I have lived on this estate my entire life. Downsizing is not an option."

"So, you would rather live in a falling down mansion than in a comfortable cottage. That is a bit elitist isn't it?"

"Someone like you wouldn't understand. At any rate, call it what you will. I have enough valuables left to last until I die, and after that what does it matter?"

"You are right about that. You certainly have enough to last until you die."

"Ah. You're here to kill me then, are you?" he asked calmly.

"I am, but first I want you to know why. You stole everything that was important to me. You took and took from everyone with no thought for what it meant to anyone but yourself."

"You make me sound like a thief. I took only what was due to me."

"That is an excuse that has been used by aristocratic thieves the world over since time began. Did you ever have pangs of conscience? Did you ever think about anyone else? Or are you so accustomed to privilege that you just feel the world owes it to you?" The visitor's face was reddening and his voice was raised in anger.

"I admit that I have been privileged in my life. But I have suffered, too. I have lost as well."

"You inherited a life that allowed you to never work a day in your life and you have thrown it away piece by piece. You stole a woman just because you could and then you threw her away, too!" The visitor raised himself from his chair and banged his fist on Harvey's desk. The effort of releasing his anger seemed to be too much for him and he quickly sat back down.

"You're getting a bit overwrought. It's causing you to…"

"You and I can be honest with each other, Harvey. You killed her. I know it and you know it and you're going to die today. So just admit it."

"That's a terrible accusation. Have you any proof? It was, after all, ruled a suicide."

The visitor took a moment to collect himself. When he spoke he was much calmer. "I know that she was a devout Catholic. You beat everything else out of her, but you couldn't change what she believed inside. She would have considered suicide to be a mortal sin that would have prevented her from being buried with the rites of her religion. And you could have paid the gards to rule her death whatever you wanted them to. So, why not get it off your chest before I kill you. They say confession is good for the soul, or do you not have a soul?"

"Alright. I may have hastened her demise. But lying with low class laborers with their dirty clothes and calloused hands? She had no right to humiliate me that way. Did she expect that I was going to stand for her having one common lover after another and do nothing about it?"

"She wasn't like that!"

"You certainly sniffed around her. Is that why you're here? You put your hands on her didn't you? She certainly didn't lie with me, well not willingly."

"Thank you for saying that. If you hadn't I might have felt some remorse for what I'm about to do, but now I can kill you with a glad heart." He got up and looked at the room and its contents. "I see you have kept this room intact. I remember the collection of swords." He pointed to one particularly ornate specimen hanging over the fireplace. "This one is supposed to have been Napoleon's, right?"

"That's the story. There's no proof of it. Is that the weapon you plan to use on me?"

"No, nothing so grand. You don't deserve it." He walked back to the desk and with his gloved hands lifted an engraved silver letter opener out of its ornately carved wooden holder. "This is beautiful. It's so shiny and sleek."

"It was my father's. A gift from my mother as I recall. It has the family crest on it."

"This is perfect. I think this is what I'll use and then I'll take it for a souvenir."

Harvey laughed quietly at the choice of weapon. "Then you can add stealing to your list of offenses."

"If they catch me and charge me with murder, I don't think they'll worry about the theft of a letter opener."

"May I ask a favor of you before I die?"

"You are in no position to ask favors."

"I can tell you are serious about taking my life, but my horse has done nothing to deserve being left to go hungry. Before you leave, will you go and feed him? He will need hay to last until Monday when my employees arrive, or at least until Sunday night. Someone might wonder why I wasn't at the ride. He needs oats as well. He has an automatic water bucket.

"I'll do that for the horse, not for you."

"Thank you. And may I leave a note for the garda to tell them to call my friend Charles to come and take the horse to his home?"

"Fine," the visitor said impatiently. "Just be quick about it."

Harvey took a pen and a piece of stationary out of the leather box on top of his desk and wrote: "Please have Charles Walker tend to my horse. I'd like him to also have this desk. The horse's papers are down under in the desk drawer. Tell him that the rest of my property will be dispersed according to my will which is in the possession of my attorney." He folded the paper in half and wrote "Garda Simms" on the front.

Harvey's visitor read the note and saw nothing to incriminate himself. He placed it back on the desk and said, "It's time." He walked around the desk and behind Harvey's chair and with no waste of movement, bent his victim's head forward to limit the blood spray and slit his throat. The blood oozed out over Harvey's threadbare smoking jacket, down his threadbare wool slacks, onto his threadbare slippers, and finally seeped into the threadbare rug beneath his feet. The visitor wrapped the letter opener in Harvey's well-worn pocket square and walked out of the house closing the kitchen door behind him as best he could.

    He went down to the lone remaining outbuilding to feed Harvey's horse, but thought, "His last words were to tell me what to do. I'm sorry horse, but I can't let him have power over me even now." So Harvey's killer walked past the barn without stopping to see to the horse and went down the back driveway to where he had parked his rental car under some trees on a patch of gravel. He was careful to leave no sign of his presence. As he left, he accelerated the car, spinning the tires so as to leave no imprint of the tread. The man felt satisfied that he had left no tire tracks, no fingerprints, no DNA. And with that, he drove away. He had done what he had wanted to do for many years and he felt relief.

1

"It's a great day for a wedding!" shouted Fiona as she entered Anna's room at Kellenwood, just outside of Graent, Ireland. She knew Anna was going to have jitters and she wanted to help prop her up. She also knew that Anna was marrying the perfect man for her. If she were to back out now, she would regret it for the rest of her life.

"Am I doing the right thing?" asked Anna.

"You are. And if I have to, I will drag you down the aisle. The yard looks so beautiful. I have never seen so many flowers in one place."

"You don't think we're rushing into this?"

"You and Shane have been together for a year. If you aren't sure by now I don't know why. I would have been sure the first time he held Winnie, or the first time he protected you from journalists or from Carl's clients. What does the man have to do to make you sure?"

"You're right, of course. The thing is that I was absolutely certain of Carl, and look what happened with him." Anna's first husband Carl had left her a year ago after embezzling large amounts of money from clients of his accounting firm. He had left the country and was now on the run in places unknown to her or to the authorities who were still looking for him. At the same time Anna had been held at gunpoint and forced to take money from her bank account to finance an escape by a murderer and his pregnant wife. The wife had been injured in the chaos that followed, and had died moments after delivering her baby. She had begged Anna with her last breaths to take care of her child. That beautiful little girl was now the light of Anna's life, and Shane loved Winnie as much as Anna did. The future looked rosy and that was what scared her.

"What about Bridget and Sarah? Are they here yet?"

"Of course. They're putting on their bride's-maids' dresses. And May is getting Winnie ready. She looks adorable, of course."

"Have you seen Shane? He didn't stay here last night. Winnie was asking about him, but we thought that we shouldn't fight tradition. He and Brian stayed at the Gentry."

"He's here. He and his hunky brother are both here. I think

he's in a hurry to make you his bride," said Bridget as she entered Anna's room. "Anna, the yard is unbelievably beautiful! The flowers are brilliant. There are people arriving quickly and filling in the seats. This is a beautiful day for a wedding." Bridget was bubbling over with enthusiasm. "And that dress looks even better today than it did the day you picked it up. I thought having a dress designed just for you was unnecessary. I know you would have looked fabulous in one off the rack. But I have to admit, it was worth it. You look extraordinary."

Anna was tall and slender with dark hair which was pulled back and hanging around her shoulders in loose curls. Her bright blue eyes were set off by the sapphire pendant that she had found among her late grandmother's treasures. It was her something old and her something blue. Her champagne colored strapless tea-length dress with its layers of chiffon, and the strapped high-heeled shoes in the same color, made the most of her best features. She stepped in front of the cheval mirror to make a final check of her appearance.

Sarah entered the room and said, "This is like a fantasy wedding day. I expect to see your fairy god-mother waving a wand around. And I could have sworn I saw a big pumpkin with some white horses hooked up to it. Seriously, this is going to be the best wedding ever. That dress is fabulous!"

"Where's Winnie?"

"May has her. You should see how cute she looks in her little dress. Anna, I promised to take care of your 'something borrowed' and here it is." She held out a bracelet of beautiful sparkling diamonds and latched it on Anna's arm.

"It's beautiful, Sarah. Thank you."

"It's one of the few pieces of jewelry I allowed Henry to buy for me before he died. So take good care of it. In a way it's as if part of him is here today, too." Sarah's husband of less than a year had died of a cancer that they knew he had before they married. But even though their marriage had been brief, it had been happy and she remembered him with great fondness.

"I won't let anything happen to it, I promise."

"I'm also in charge of the 'something new' as well, but I have saved that for later."

At that moment, Charles, Fiona's husband, appeared in the

doorway and said, "I think it's about time we headed for the altar. Are you ladies just about ready?"

"Charles, as my attorney, do you think I'm doing the right thing marrying Shane?" asked Anna.

Charles looked at his wife and said, "Is she serious?"

"No, my darling, she just wants to make sure she gets a prize as wonderful as you. I told her there was no chance of that."

"Of course not, but Shane will do. After all the two of you have been through together, I'm surprised you even have to ask. And you look even more beautiful than usual," he said planting a kiss on her cheek. "And I say that not as your attorney, but as your friend. And by the way, you look ravishing," he said to Fiona.

"Thank you, sir. We're on our way. Is Shane out of the house?"

"Yes. He and his brother are standing in wait at the altar."

"Then it's time," said Fiona. "You go now and then Bridget and I will follow, then Sarah and finally Anna. Let's hurry before she loses her nerve."

And so the little parade departed in the prearranged order, into the hall, out the side door, and down to the lawn. Arbors had been placed over the pathway and covered with hanging flowers. The lane was well-defined and led to a clearing where chairs had been set up for the one hundred or so guests. They walked down the aisle and when Anna caught sight of Shane, looking dashing in his black tuxedo, all of her doubts and fears vanished. She felt ridiculous about having had any reservations. He was beaming at her and when she got to his side and handed her bouquet off to Sarah, he took her hands in his and gave her a light peck on the cheek. The vows were traditional, the service was short, and they exchanged platinum Claddagh rings, hers set with a sparkling diamond. When they turned to walk back the way Anna had just come, they heard a small voice say, "Mommy and Daddy." With a rush of emotion, Shane reached down and picked up Winnie from May's lap and carried her with them up the aisle. They were a ready-made modern family.

It was a wonderful day. The food was delicious and plentiful. Shane's construction company crew had made perfectly leveled dance floors out of hard-wood, and placed them securely on the lawn. There were two bands taking turns, one a rock cover band

and the other a traditional Irish pub band. The music didn't stop all night and the guests and the couple all enjoyed themselves immensely. When Anna and Shane danced the first dance, he held Winnie and twirled his two girls across the floor. Charles cut in and Shane took the opportunity to carry the drowsy Winnie to May and Robert, her adoptive grandparents and Anna's live-in hired help.

"Anna, this has been a lovely evening for everyone. Now, don't you feel just a bit silly for having had doubts earlier on?" asked Charles.

"I felt silly the moment I saw him standing there waiting for me with that beautiful smile on that beautiful face. I never thought I could be this happy again. Charles, you have been so helpful throughout the last year with the problems Carl left me, and also with the adoption process. I don't think I would be here right now if it hadn't been for you and I want to thank you."

"I was happy to do it. You deserve all the happiness you have. I did want to ask you one thing. Did you invite Harvey to the wedding?"

"I did. He's not here?"

"No. You set the large table for the riding club, and his seat is empty. I wonder if he didn't come because he's still feeling some loyalty to Carl."

"I don't think so. He called me the day his invitation arrived in the mail and he seemed truly happy for me. He said he was looking forward to the day, and he has said several times in the last year that Carl had been horrible to do what he did to me. I'm sure he intended to be here. I hope there's nothing wrong."

"He's been a bit under the weather, but nothing serious. I'm sure he's fine. I'll talk to him tomorrow on the ride. By the way, you will be missing two rides. I think that's your maximum for the year."

"I will miss it. We even thought of waiting until Monday, but with Shane's work schedule, he felt he should go sooner rather than later."

"I wish I could talk you into waiting just one more day, but I'm sure you have reservations in place and so forth. You will both be missed. And I will see to Harvey. If I don't get a chance to say so before you go," and he was able to say it to both of them as Shane returned to the floor, "have a wonderful trip. And let us know the second you return. My wife will not be fit to live with while you're gone."

The party began to break up at 1:00 in the morning as people tired themselves out on the dance floor. Many of the guests were going on a long horse-back ride in the early morning, so they left, all of them giving their best wishes to Mr. and Mrs. Anderson. Fiona, Bridget and Sarah encircled her and gave her a group hug, wished her a wonderful vacation and promised that her home, the Graent Arts Center that Anna and Shane had built, and even her friends would be okay in her absence, as long as she wasn't gone for too long. Sarah exchanged her diamond bracelet for the 'something new,' a slightly risqué negligée that was so small as to fit inside a tiny gift bag that she seemed to have pulled out of the air. Anna shared a laugh with her friends about the gift, and then she turned and threw her bouquet behind her directly into the arms of her friend Sarah. Finally, at the end of a wonderful day and a great party, the newly-wed couple went upstairs to their first night of marriage, and with all of their already-packed luggage on the floor around them, they drifted off to sleep and woke in the morning ready to start on a two-week trip to Scotland with a one year old baby in tow.

But in the light of the morning on a day that looked like perfect weather for a ride, the two of them agreed that they could leave one day later than planned, that Winnie needed a day of rest after the chaos of the previous day, and that they also weren't ready for hours in the car. So on a whim, they decided to put on not their traveling clothes, but their riding clothes. They called the stable and asked Robert to get their horses ready for the Sunday ride.

2

This Sunday's ride was at the home of the Chases. They were an older couple who had fallen on hard times. They had lived in their current home north of Graent for two years having sold a much larger home in Dublin. They had both worked hard all their lives and built a company that supported them and their three children. When they sold their business and downsized to the cottage in Graent, they bought a pair of carriage horses and joined the riding club, though they didn't ride; they drove their perfectly matched pair of black and white Gypsy Horses hitched to a custom-made two-wheeled cart with shocks and cushions enough to make even the most challenging course comfortable for its passengers. Their finances suffered after some health issues and they had come close to losing their home. They had recovered enough to maintain their lifestyle, but without the extras they had looked forward to, such as traveling and expanding their home. As a result their brunch was not spectacular and the champagne was donated to them, but the mood was light still and though they had lost much of their money, they had lost none of their good friends.

The day promised to be a great success as it always was when the weather cooperated. The three friends got ready to ride together, talking about how they were missing one of their group, but just as they were walking to the house for brunch they recognized the white trailer pulled by the red Range Rover and knew it was Anna and Shane. They were excited to see them, but wondered why they hadn't left on their trip. "We were getting ready to leave this morning and decided that we just couldn't miss two rides," said Anna as she caught up to her three friends. "We definitely won't be here next week, but we thought it wouldn't make that big a difference if we left tomorrow instead of today."

The four friends enjoyed the breakfast together as Shane and Charles talked about the upcoming drive. Most of the conversation this day was about the wedding the day before. The consensus was that it was one of the most beautiful weddings anyone had ever attended. The members of the group were excited to tell the newlyweds how much they enjoyed the celebration. And then the Chases led the group out onto flat lands accessible by their horse-drawn cart. It was a sight to see, the two elderly people with a red plaid rug over their laps, with him at the reins, and the long mane and fetlocks of the two paint horses flowing in the breeze. When the ride was done and Anna and Shane had driven off, the three remaining friends decided that while Anna was gone they needed to keep up with their friend therapy, so lunch was planned for Tuesday at the Gentry Hotel. They loaded their horses for the trip home, and went off in their respective directions.

When Fiona and Charles arrived home they put away their horses for the night. They brought the other two horses in their herd into stalls all ready for them and they returned to the house. As Fiona was dealing with the nightly ritual of Lunar and Solar, their two Border-Collie dogs, Charles said, "If you don't mind, I think I'm going to take a ride over to Harvey's house. I don't like that he didn't go to Anna's wedding and he didn't ride today. He may be in need of help. I know he's complained of feeling unwell lately and I just feel that if I don't go and check on him I won't be able to sleep tonight."

"Oh God. I was so happy to see Shane and Anna that I didn't even notice that he wasn't there. Would you like me to go with you?"

"No." He kissed her on the cheek and said, "I know you're tired. Take a hot bath. If all is well I'll be back shortly. If not, if there's anything I need to do to help him, I'll call you and let you know."

Fiona told him to hurry home and when the dogs were safely back inside the house, she went up the stairs, while Charles, still in his riding clothes and boots, went out the back door and got his car from the garage for the ride to Harvey Glavin's house. He arrived there within fifteen minutes to find the house in total darkness. The ride had ended after 6:00, and it had taken Charles and Fiona at least two hours to load the trailer, return home and take care of their horses. Add to that the time it took him to drive to Harvey's and that made the time close to 9:00. He found the flashlight that he always kept in the glove box of his car and used it to light his way to the house. He knocked several times, and getting no answer, he took the spare key from where Harvey kept it under a paving stone, and let himself in. He found the light switch just inside the hallway and turned it on.

He called Harvey's name and heard no response. What he did hear was a buzzing sound coming from Harvey's study and he smelled an unmistakable odor in the air. He entered the room through the doorway off the front foyer and turned on the light. What he saw sickened him. There was his old friend Harvey, seated at his desk, his head slumped forward and his chin resting on his chest, with flies buzzing around an open wound that sliced his neck from ear to ear. Charles was an attorney and had had enough experience with cases of unattended deaths to know that he should touch nothing. Still his first instinct was to go to Harvey and try to help, even though he knew that there was nothing that could be done for him. With a heavy heart he took his mobile phone from his pocket, and dialed garda headquarters in nearby Graent to report the suspicious death. He gave the dispatcher his name and Harvey's address. He stepped into the foyer and called Fiona to tell her the news and that he wouldn't be home for some time, and then he filled the time until the garda arrived by going back to look over what was surely a murder scene.

As he walked down the hall toward the kitchen he noticed a broken mug with sticky tea puddled on the floor. It looked as if someone had walked through the liquid and left tracks on the floor going in the direction of the kitchen. He was careful not to disturb them with his own boots. He reached into the kitchen and shone his torch making the rounds of the room. There were the signs of Harvey's having made his own tea. The canister was sitting on the table, the sugar bowl was still open and the spoon he had used was on the table as well. Beyond the counter top, Charles could see without going into the room that the kitchen door had been splintered.

He had left the front door wide open and Garda Simms entered calling his name. They greeted one another with Charles reminding him that they had met before. Garda Simms had been on the case when Anna had found a dead body in the trunk of a car that had been left in her grandfather's yard. He had also been helpful after Anna had been taken hostage by the killer. Charles had acted on Anna's behalf and he had developed a respect for the gard.

"Have you been wandering around in here, Mr. Walker?"

"I have," said Charles, "but I have been careful. Would you like to know what I've seen?"

"Yes, I would." Garda Simms also remembered Charles' contributions to the previous case and that he had great admiration for him as an attorney and as a man to be trusted.

"I came in the front door with a key Harvey had hidden. He showed it to me a while ago when he started having some minor health issues, in case I needed to get in here in an emergency. He has people working for him, but he's quite alone in the evenings and on the weekends. There are two entrances to his study. I went in through the door from the front foyer and found his body. I also found some clues to what happened, if you'll follow me to the hallway nearer to the other entrance to the room." He led Garda Simms to the spot. "I believe that Harvey had just made himself a cup of tea. I think he was carrying it to his study when someone broke in through the kitchen door. You can see that it has been splintered if you look through the kitchen. This surprised him and he dropped his cup on the floor. He was probably forced by his intruder to go into the study through the other door that comes off the hallway." He then led the garda into the study. "Harvey sat at his desk while the other person sat in this chair. It usually sits over there by the lamp table where you can still see the indentations in the rug, but it's been moved here so the person could face him. They sat here and probably talked until the killer walked around behind him and slit his throat."

"I don't see a weapon."

Charles indicated a carved wooden fixture sitting atop the desk. "Harvey had an engraved sterling-silver letter opener sitting on this holder. It had belonged to his father. It's missing. I think that was the murder weapon."

Garda Simms looked around the room at the sword collection mounted on the wall. "I see many weapons that would have been much easier to use to kill a man. Why wouldn't he have used one of those?"

"I have a theory about that. If I hated someone enough to do this to him, I would not honor him with a death by an antique sword. These are collectors' items, each of them extremely valuable. I think the killer is saying that Harvey isn't worthy of them. I also think that this was personal. I think the killer wanted to be up close and in contact with him."

"Wouldn't that make a struggle more of a possibility? Why take that risk?"

"I see no signs of a struggle. My guess is that Harvey knew he had no chance and he sat here and had a conversation with this person, knowing that when they were done talking, he would be killed. Harvey was cut from a different cloth than the rest of us. I can hear him saying, 'Alright, let's get this over with.' The killer walks behind him and calmly slits his throat and takes the letter opener with him as a souvenir, or perhaps to make sure you don't have access to his DNA. Then he turns off the lights and walks out the way he came, but he didn't think to avoid the tea spilled on the floor. With the lights off in the study and the lack of good lighting in the hall, the killer might not even have seen it. He might also have wanted to leave in a hurry after the job was done, so he wasn't paying attention to where he was stepping. Harvey used a lot of sugar and cream so it made sticky footprints."

"We can't get too excited about that. They could be Harvey's."

"There's clearly tread in these prints. Harvey is wearing his house slippers. They're the same ones he's had all the time I've known him. If there ever had been tread on them, it's gone now."

"And what about your boots?"

"These are my riding boots. As you can see there is no tread on them except for the pattern on the heel." He lifted his left foot to demonstrate to Simms that his footprints would not have made the marks that they saw going from the hallway to the outside kitchen door. "And I made certain that I did not get near to the spill."

"How is it that you came over here today, if you don't mind my asking?"

"Harvey was supposed to ride with us today. He never misses a ride. Also, he didn't attend Shane and Anna's wedding yesterday, and I think he really wanted to be there. So I took my wife home after the ride and told her that I needed to check on him."

"Anna and Shane married yesterday?"

"They did."

"I'm glad to hear it. They made a nice couple and excellent

parents for that little girl." Simms had been in the hospital when the baby's mother died, and as a father himself, had worried about the child's future. "I guess that helps us to narrow down the time of death to sometime before he would have left for the wedding."

"I think I can do better than that. Harvey was a creature of habit for one thing. Also, he was of the opinion that no one could fix his tea to suit him. He mentioned more than once that his housekeeper's last job of the day was to brew a pot of tea and that he would fix it himself as soon as she left. Her day ends at 5:00. I would say that fixes the time of the break-in at however long after that time that it would have taken him to fix the tea and walk just this far from the kitchen."

"And you don't think this could have been his Saturday morning tea?"

"No. On the weekends he went to the pub in town for all of his meals. He was useless in the kitchen and would have starved before he fixed anything to eat or brew tea. I suggested one time that he keep some things on hand that he could just pick up and eat and he wouldn't hear of it. He liked to be served. Fixing his own tea after someone else brewed it was as domesticated as he ever got."

"What is the name of his housekeeper?"

"That I don't know. 'That wretched woman' was what he called her," he said with a chuckle. "Harvey didn't have people over except when it was his turn to host the Sunday ride, and even then no one was invited inside the house. I think he was ashamed of its condition and the selling of his valuables. I came here more often than most I guess, but I was his attorney and he wanted me to know where things were, including the extra key. Even then I was only asked to come here on the weekends when his employees were not around."

"Employees, plural?"

"There was a groundskeeper. He didn't work on weekends, either. And no, I don't know his name. Harvey was my friend, but I knew him to be a bit of a snob. His employees were just that to him, not real people with names."

"I'm sure we can find out who they are." Garda Simms then walked down the hall and into the study. He saw a sheet of folded note paper on top of the desk, used his pen to flip it over and read it without picking it up. "It looks like the killer let him write a note. It's addressed to me and says, 'Please have Charles Walker tend to my horse. I'd like him to also have this desk. The horse's papers are down under in the desk drawer. Tell him that the rest of my property will be dispersed according to my will which is in the possession of my attorney.' Did you know about this?"

"I didn't. I guess I was too upset by the sight of Harvey's throat being cut to pay attention to what was on the desk. I'm still in a bit of shock. I hadn't thought about the horse. If you don't mind I would like to check on him. If Harvey's been like this for a couple of days, and it looks as if he has, the horse could be very hungry. Do you need me for anything else?"

"No, my team is pulling in the driveway now, so you can go see to the horse. You know, if these swords are as valuable as you say, then we can probably rule out robbery."

"Not only that, but some of the paintings and the first edition books in this room are extremely valuable as well."

"Right. If you wouldn't mind, I'd like you to go to the station tomorrow and fill out a statement. Can you do that?"

"I will. I'll be there early in the morning before I go to the office if that's good for you. If I'm to take care of the horse, I'd like to come and get him tomorrow. It will be easier for me to take care of him at my house. If this paper doesn't hold up, I'll give him back to his rightful owner, but in the meantime, I'll have him in my barn."

"That's fine. I imagine that I'll be working overnight so when you come in early I'll still be there."

"I'll see you then."

3

Charles drove his car to the barn, and shining his headlights to help him find his way in the dark, entered through the far doors which he knew to be nearer to the horse's stall. As he had done in the house he used his flash-light to find the light switch on the wall and he turned it on. He expected Big Tim to be anxious for food, but instead he found him eating from a nearly full hay rack with some of his oats left in his grain box. Charles noticed that the stall was in need of cleaning, but otherwise the horse seemed to have been recently cared for. He wondered if the killer had taken the time to care for the horse before he left. That didn't seem like the actions of a murderer. He felt certain that Harvey had been dead for some time and that if he had been the one to feed Big Tim, he also would have cleaned his stall.

It was too late in the evening to do that job now. After all, the horse would be leaving here in the morning anyway. He poured a generous amount of clean oats in the grain box in the corner in case he was delayed in the morning. He checked to make sure that the water bucket was working and that it was clean. Big Tim seemed to be alright for the night, so Charles turned off the lights, closed up the barn and returned to his car.

He drove by Harvey's house and let Garda Simms know the situation and then went home. Fiona met him at the door. "How are you holding up? It must have been horrible to find him that way. Can I get you a cup of coffee or would you like something stronger?"

"Brandy would be nice." She poured him a generous drink and handed it to him as he settled into an overstuffed chair in the sitting room with their two dogs at his feet. They could tell he was upset about something and they wanted to be near him if he needed them. He took a long sip of the hot liquid and lay his head back on the chair.

"You look exhausted. Do you want to talk about it?"

"I'm too tired to talk about it, but I have to talk about it. Does that make sense?"

"Of course. Tell me everything."

He told her about going there and the house being dark. He told her about finding the body and the spilled tea. He told her about the broken door. He did not tell her about the flies. He wished he could have been spared that detail, so he wasn't going to inflict that visual image on her. He also told her about the horse and that they would have to go in the morning to get him. Then he told her about the note.

"It's odd, really. I didn't think much of it at first, but on the way home I had time to consider the wording of the note. I can understand his wanting me to take care of the horse, but why did he want me to have that monster of a desk? He would have known I wouldn't have a place for it. The note he wrote almost sounded like a will, but he also knew that I would know about his will. I'm the one who drew up the latest version of it. I'm too tired to think about what it all means. It turns out that finding a dear friend with his throat slit is exhausting. I have to get up early to get the horse and then I have to fit a trip to garda headquarters into my day tomorrow. I already had a busy day planned."

"I can take care of the horse if you want me to. Big Tim is a huge animal, but he's a pussy-cat, so getting him ready and loading him into the trailer will be easy. I'll call Bridget to help. That way you can check that job off your list."

"I am going to take you up on that. Thanks Fi."

"I think I'll call Bridget and Sarah now and let them know the latest. They're more likely to stay up late than to get up early. I had called both of them to tell them about Harvey, so I would guess that they are both finding it hard to sleep tonight anyway. They were understandably upset. Why don't you go up and take a hot shower and get some sleep. I'll be up as soon as I have made the arrangements with the girls. I don't know if I should call Anna. What do you think?"

Charles drained his glass and said, "The hot shower is a great idea, but no, I wouldn't call Anna. Let her have her honeymoon. My guess is that it won't be on the news before they leave in the morning. They were planning to get an early start. Hurry on up. I think I'd get to sleep better with you next to me." He took the stairs slowly with the two dogs at his feet.

"I'll be right there." She made the two phone calls and set up a time for Bridget to be at her house in the morning. Sarah said that if they had any trouble, to call and she would bring her two stable men to help. That done she checked the doors to see that they were locked, turned off the lights, and with a heavy heart, she climbed the stairs.

4

"Fiona, are you awake?" asked Charles as he gently nudged her shoulder. "I have to leave now if I'm going to give my statement at the Garda station and make it to work on time for my first appointment of the day, and you have a horse to pick up." He had already been up for some time and was dressed in a suit and ready to leave.

"Oh, I'm sorry. I wanted to be up in time to fix you some breakfast."

"Don't worry. I'll stop on my way to see Garda Simms and get some coffee and a scone."

Fiona got up and put on a robe. She walked Charles downstairs to the door and told him she would call him when she had taken care of Harvey's horse. He left the house and went straight to his arranged meeting with Garda Simms and then on to the office for his previously scheduled busy day. Fiona took care of her own animals and had the trailer hooked up to the Range Rover by the time Bridget arrived. She called Charles later that morning as soon as Big Tim was in his new stall and she was able to give him a good report. "Big Tim is here and in his stall. We gave him some food before we got him ready for the trip. We also couldn't leave his stall the way it was so we cleaned it before we left. Harvey was meticulous when it came to Big Tim's stall and we felt like we had to leave it spotless."

"That was good of you. How is he settling in at our place?"

"He's fine. We fed him again. He smells the other horses, but he's been around other horses before and stabled in other people's barns, so he doesn't seem to think anything of it. He probably thinks he's here for a slightly delayed Sunday ride."

"Good job, you. I'll be home for dinner. It's going to be a rough day. I find myself thinking of Harvey and losing concentration."

"The day will be over before you know it. We'll have a quiet evening. It'll do you good." They said their good-byes and she joined Bridget in the stable.

Fiona's stable was built over one hundred and fifty years

earlier of grey stone with red brick quoining at the corners and around the doors and windows. It consisted of four buildings facing each other across a cobble-stone court-yard in a quadrant with a driveway that circled through and out again around the western building. The horse stalls were in the eastern building and consisted of eight stalls in a row, each of which opened into the courtyard. The front stall doors were Dutch and allowed the horses to see what was going on around them when the top halves were left open during the day. There were rear doors as well to allow the residents of the six center stalls to go out to the common meadow in good weather. The two end stalls opened into strip pastures to separate the horses in them from the others, and they placed Harvey's horse in one of those end stalls so he could go out and become accustomed to the other horses across the fence before joining them in the larger field. The western barn contained the office and tack room. At the north end of the court-yard was a large wooden building for storage of hay and at the south was another large wooden building which housed the horse trailer and the Range Rover they used to pull it, as well as a small farm tractor and all the necessary equipment for taking care of horses.

Harvey's 17 hand Thoroughbred made horse number five for them. After he was settled in and seemed comfortable in his space, Bridget helped Fiona check on the other four horses to see how they felt about a newcomer in their midst. Fiona then asked, "How about going back to the house and having some breakfast? I have some really good cranberry scones from the bakery in town."

"That sounds good to me," said Bridget. They walked to the house and entered through the backdoor of an addition Fiona and Charles had added to the house a few years after the initial purchase. The two dogs were wagging their tails so hard that their bodies were folding in half. Bridget made sure to give each of them an equal amount of attention and then followed Fiona into the kitchen.

The house was stone like the stables and was a two-story square box with four rooms up and four rooms down, with an attached two car garage leading into the kitchen. Inside, each room was spacious with a high ceiling, making the generous sized rooms seem even larger. In spite of being structurally sound, the house had been a disaster when they first viewed it, but they loved it and saw potential in it. They had been married for a year and were tired of living in a small four room apartment and they were also tired of living in the city. They both loved Dublin, but they wanted the peace and quiet of the countryside. They made certain of the plumbing, the roof, and the electricity before they moved in and they had experts deal with the windows, the floors and also the ceilings, which they left tall and lofty. Then they moved in and went to work themselves, finishing one room at a time. They removed old paper and painted the walls, they stripped the wood trim and doors and stained them so that the natural beauty of the wood showed through, and they decorated the rooms with great care and good taste. They lived on the first floor using what would eventually become a study/office as a bedroom until they could move upstairs. They spent many Saturday afternoons traveling the country looking for quality furniture and decorative pieces at bargain prices. Most of the house was outfitted with sturdy and functional second-hand items of such character that they were kept even after the couple could afford to replace them. Their home was beautiful and it reflected their personal tastes. The single story back addition gave them a lighter airier dining area and sun-room looking out onto the rolling hills beyond their backyard. In comparison to the homes of many of their friends, their home was small and less ostentatious, but they loved it.

    Fiona didn't have live-in help like some of her friends. She had left her secretarial job at a rival law firm after she and Charles married, and she took pleasure in the daily chores of cooking and taking care of her own home, and of course, the animals. She even cut the lawn on her tractor mower. She had someone come in to clean the house and do the laundry once a week, and she had someone else to trim the planting beds, prune the trees and do the labor intensive tasks related to taking care of a substantial yard. She and Charles spent their Saturdays dealing with all the other homeowner details and on Sundays they rode with their friends. She loved her husband and she loved her life. Sometimes she thought it would be nice to have a child or two, and then she would go to shop for food and see what mothers went through with children screaming and running amok, and she would say she and Charles had made the right choice to remain childless. She would leave the rearing of children to people with more patience than she had. She would stick to dogs and horses.

When she had made the coffee and placed some scones on her Belleek plates, she let the dogs outside. She called Bridget in to get her cup and plate and they went to the new addition for breakfast. The main topic of discussion was, of course, what had happened to their friend. "Who would want to kill Harvey?" asked Bridget. "I've always thought of him as a harmless old gentleman who never went out and about enough to make enemies. I thought that his circle of acquaintances consisted of the Sunday riding group only."

"True, I feel the same way. But we never really know people, do we? Sometimes people act completely differently in social situations than they do otherwise. We also have no idea what he was like before he became old and harmless. Sometimes these things are the result of something that happened many years earlier. I know he was in the army and fought in the war, and he was married for a short time, and I know that his mother died when he was young and his father when he was in his twenties, which was when he inherited his estate. I don't know much more than that about his life and he was never one to volunteer information. He was of the age that he kept himself to himself, as they say."

"So you think it was someone he knew long ago?"

"I hope so. I have no reason for thinking that, but I want it to be someone from his distant past, because if it isn't, it could be someone we know and I wouldn't like that."

"What about a simple robbery? He had sold many of his antiques, but he still had many items of value left."

"Charles said that all of those valuable swords and his paintings and books were still there. I would expect that any thief would have taken those. He thinks they have all but ruled out robbery."

"I know that of all the people in our riding club, Harvey was closest to Charles and then Charles was the one to find him. How is he handling that? It had to be upsetting for him."

"Charles is always the same. He is friendly and caring and upbeat at all times. Last night he was sad and stricken in a way that I have never seen him. It was such a shock. He was concerned about Harvey because he missed not only the Sunday ride, but Anna's wedding as well. It was so unlike him to do that. He said it looked as if Harvey's body had been there for a while. He didn't go into detail, but I got the impression that the condition of the body was disturbing."

"When I worked as a nurse I dealt with several deaths. Even in a hospital setting with people we knew were going to die, it was still upsetting to walk into a room and discover a body. I'm sorry he had to go through that. I still can't get some of those images out of my mind all these years later. Look, I'm sorry to leave you with this, but I have to go," said Bridget. "I wish I could stay and visit, but Daniel and I have some things to deal with this morning. Let me know if you learn anything, and will you tell Charles how sorry I am that he had to go through that?"

"I will. Thank you so much for all your help with Big Tim. And if nothing comes up before then, we have lunch at the Gentry tomorrow."

"Yes. I will talk to you then if not before."

Fiona cleaned up the kitchen and put everything away and then changed into more suitable clothes for shopping. She let the dogs in and went to the market to buy what she needed to fix Charles his favorite dinner and try to make him forget the image of his good friend that he surely had stuck in his mind.

5

Charles got home at 6:00 and dinner was almost ready for him. Fiona had taken care of the animals so he could relax when he arrived, and she told him to go upstairs and change into his favorite flannel pants and a tee-shirt, because it would be just the two of them for the evening. When he came downstairs to the greetings of the two dogs, she had a Guinness poured for him and he could smell dinner cooking. "You made lasagna," he said as he dropped onto the sofa.

"I did," she said as she settled next to him and put her head on his shoulder.

"Are you taking care of me?"

"I am."

"I don't need anyone to take care of me, but if you insist on it I will allow it just this once, especially if it involves my favorite meal and my favorite person in the whole world."

"Do you remember the first time we had lasagna together?" she asked brushing a lock of hair off his forehead.

"It was on our first date. Why do you think I like it so much? It was the first day of the rest of my life, as the saying goes."

Charles had just gotten a job with one of the most prestigious law firms in Dublin. He was expecting a firm from the other side of the city to send him some papers. He did not expect that the person delivering them to him would be a tall red-head with a super model's body and bright green eyes. When he took the papers from her, their fingers touched and neither of them could let go. They stood there looking as if they were playing tug-of-war until he asked, "Can I have your number?" She gave it to him and he called her that night. He said, "I have to go out of town for the weekend, but may I take you to dinner Monday night when I get back?" She answered yes, and they went out to a small intimate Italian restaurant for lasagna. Neither of them ever looked at another member of the opposite sex again.

"You told me your life story that night."

"I did do a lot of the talking, didn't I?"

"I wanted to hear it all."

The Sunday Rider

Charles and his parents and two brothers had lived in Belfast, and when the fighting began, his parents couldn't bear to send their children off to school in the morning, not knowing if they would make it home at the end of the day. So early one Saturday, they packed their belongings into a dilapidated trailer, loaded their kids and their dog into the car, and they drove to the western part of Northern Ireland to the farm where Charles' father had lived as a boy. His parents had died and left it to him, but until the troubles started he had had no interest in it. When they arrived, the house was a wreck and the two small barns were worse, but there were no bombs or soldiers with guns there. They all pitched in and worked hard to make the house livable and the barns usable. They raised produce to sell and both parents found jobs in the town nearby.

They managed to make a success of the place and by the time Charles was ready to go to University, his two older brothers had both graduated and gotten jobs as teachers, one of math and one of history. Charles assumed he would follow suit until one day after working at his part-time job at the local hardware store, he went to the diner in town to treat himself to a piece of pie and a glass of milk. A man in his late fifties sat down beside him and they started to talk. The older man was impressed by Charles' intelligence and maturity, both good qualities for an attorney to have. By the time he had paid for his pie and milk, they had come to an arrangement. Charles would study law. The older man would subsidize his living expenses and any tuition or other costs beyond his regular university education, and Charles would return when he qualified and join the older man's law firm, the only one in town. He would work with him during his vacations to learn the way the firm functioned and when Charles was finished with his education, he would have a job that would provide him with a good future.

The older man was true to his word and several years later Charles walked into the office on his last day of summer vacation and said, "I can't believe I'm about to start my last year of school."

"I look forward to having you join me. There's plenty of work for the two of us as you well know, and with you here I might finally be able to slow down a bit."

Charles had gone off to Belfast and two weeks into the school year, he received a call from his father telling him that his benefactor had died suddenly. Because of the timing, and because people in the town couldn't wait to deal with their legal issues until Charles became qualified to practice law, someone else opened a firm in town and Charles' future was no longer certain. He had worried that he would be without a placement when he graduated, but he sent out numerous applications and found a spot in one of the largest law firms in Dublin. There he was when the beautiful Fiona walked into his life.

At the end of the evening Charles realized that he had monopolized the conversation. "I told you my life story tonight. When do I get to hear yours?"

"How about tomorrow evening?"

"I'll pick you up at 7:00."

And so Fiona told her story at dinner the next night. Hers was much different from Charles'. Her alcoholic father had died when she was ten years old. The family could never count on his pay check and there were times when food and rent were hard to come by. Her mother was never physically harmed by him, but when he was drunk he was often verbally abusive and the threats of violence were always there in the tone of his voice. Her mother was released from this torment by his death, but she had to raise her daughter on her own. She found a job, worked hard, and was Fiona's best friend until she died when Fiona was eighteen years old. There would be no university education for her. She needed to find work, so when a friend of her mother's recommended her for a job as a secretary in a Dublin law firm, she was elated. She found a flat by answering an add posted in the local paper, and moved in with two roommates, one of whom would remain her very best friend long after they both married. When she told Bridget that a handsome young lawyer had asked her to dinner, Bridget could see that Fiona was smitten. "Go get him," she had said.

"That's an odd thing to say," said Fiona.

"I can see in your eyes that you have set your sights on this man. I know you don't see yourself the way everyone else sees you, but you are one of the most beautiful women I know, and also one of the best people I know, and if you go after this guy, he doesn't stand a chance."

On the evening of their second date, when he walked her to the door of her apartment, he said, "I don't know how you feel about me, Fiona, but after knowing you for such a short time, I can't imagine ever letting you go." She leaned toward him and gave him a kiss on the cheek and that was that. Any time apart was unbearable for both of them and so they married after a six month engagement and never regretted it.

They both remembered all of this as they sat on the sofa drinking Guinness and thinking about how far they had come. A timer went off in the kitchen and Fiona went in to check on the meal. She called to him that it was ready and he joined her in the dining room for a salad, her home-made lasagna, hot rolls, with lemon bars and coffee for dessert. It wasn't enough to make them forget that they'd just lost a dear friend, but it allowed them for a short time to think of more pleasant memories.

6

Charles had a particularly busy schedule on Tuesday, so after talking about the day ahead over breakfast, he went to the office and Fiona called the dogs and went to the stable. She had a new resident to tend to.

She fed her own horses and shooed them all out to the pasture so she could clean their stalls. She thought she should spend some quiet time with the new horse in the stable. She brought him out into the yard and tied him to a ring set into the wall of the stable. When she was finished cleaning and filling the stall with shavings, she gave him a good brushing and led him through the stall and out the back door and into the pasture. He was accustomed to being alone so segregating him in the end stall wasn't uncomfortable for him, but he could hear and smell the other horses in the barn, and horses are social creatures. Fiona knew that the sooner she assimilated him into the group, the sooner he would be truly comfortable in his new home. She took her time because doing this hard work was pleasure for her. She never took her mobile to the barn so as not to be disturbed. The people close to her knew the number for the land line phone in the tack room and used it only in case of emergency. She turned her radio up loud and used the time doing her shoveling and wheel-barrowing and giving each one a quick brush in turn, to do her best thinking.

Of course her thoughts this morning were consumed with the murder of Harvey Glavin. Who would want to kill him? Was it someone they all knew or someone from Harvey's past? What did they really know about his life? He was so much older than they were, and her circle of friends only came to know him within the last ten or twelve years. The riding group seemed to be the only friends he had currently, but he had been married for a time. Could the murderer be someone he didn't even know? And what about that note that Charles had told her about? It made perfect sense that he would want to see to the care of his horse before he died, and it also made sense to give the horse to Charles. But what about that huge desk? There had to be some reason for that. The part about his property sounded as if were writing a will, but he had filed his will with Charles years ago and made no secret of the fact that his prodigal brother would be left with the task of unloading the heavy burden of that house and property. It was almost as if he were trying to leave them a clue to his murderer without letting the killer know about it. It was a puzzle, and no one she knew was smarter or better at solving puzzles than Bridget.

She finished in the stables, said good-bye to Big Tim, and returned to the house to get ready to go to lunch. She would be meeting Sarah and Bridget. She knew Sarah would dress for comfort and Bridget would dress to hide what she saw as too much weight. Fiona had grown up not knowing what it was like to buy expensive clothes, and now even though she could certainly afford to shop in the trendiest of stores, she still usually bought second hand, only now it was called vintage. She dressed in a comfortable elastic-waist skirt and a loose fitting sweater over a camisole. She wore wedge sandals and carried a matching purse. She felt like a combination of Sarah's and Bridget's styles. She closed the dogs inside the house and told them to be good and then she went to get her car from the garage.

She drove her Audi convertible to the Gentry and handed over the keys to the garage attendant. She went up to the main floor marveling at the old-world beauty of the place. She had been here more times than she could count since she and Charles first had dinner here, but she found it to be one of the most beautiful buildings in Dublin and she never tired of taking in every detail. The lobby was immense with tall white Corinthian columns providing support and dividing the room into conversation areas. The front desk was made of dark wood trimmed with brass and polished to a mirror-like shine. The furniture was from an earlier time, but was meticulously maintained, and the black and gray checked marble floor was crisp and clean and had a sound when people walked on it that suggested opulence, if such a thing were possible. She found her way to the dining room beyond the bar and opposite the desk, and joined her friends who were already seated. There was a glass of wine waiting for her.

When Fiona had taken her seat, and the waiter had placed her napkin in her lap, Bridget raised her glass and said, "To dear friends both present and absent, and to the meal we are about to have together."

Fiona and Sarah said in unison, "To friends," and Fiona said, "To poor dear Harvey, and to Anna on her honeymoon, and may it be as beautiful as that wedding. She deserves a man like Shane. He's not only handsome, but he also truly loves her and Winnie. He's just what she needed after what Carl did to her."

"The wedding really was beautiful. The weather was great, the food was spectacular, and that cake," said Bridget.

Sarah added, "It was both beautiful and intimate as well. It was so Anna."

"It was perfect. And Winnie, whom I miss terribly already, by the way, was adorable in her little dress and so well behaved. It almost makes me think about having kids someday."

"Bridget! I've never heard you say anything about having kids. Are you actually planning on it?"

"No. The way things are for me right now, having kids is the last thing on my mind. I'm just saying she's a sweetie. I think we can all agree on that."

And of course, they did.

Sarah asked, "Did you two get Big Tim taken care of?"

Fiona said, "He's a sweetie, too. He was easy to deal with and he has settled in nicely. I gave him a little extra TLC this morning."

"I just can't get over Harvey's death. It was such a shock," said Sarah. "I can't understand why anyone would want to kill Harvey. When I first came to Graent and married Henry, Harvey was one of the first to make me feel welcome. That was before I met you two and Anna, of course. If it hadn't been for him I wouldn't have worked so hard to learn to ride so that I could join you all on Sundays. He invited me even though Henry couldn't go anymore."

"I've been wondering if the killer might be someone from his past," said Fiona. She told them about the questions she had had while she was doing her barn chores that morning. The other two had had similar thoughts. Sarah was considered the detective of the group after having once solved a thirty year old murder mystery. Bridget was the smart one, the one who thought outside the box. Fiona thought that maybe among the three of them they would be able to figure out the meaning of the note Harvey had left.

"Let's not get into the sort of trouble that Anna and Sarah did when they got too close to a murderer. I think it is fine to figure out the message, but we have gotten too close to danger before and we need to agree beforehand to stay safe," said Bridget.

"I definitely don't want anyone to hold a knife to my neck again, so we need to be careful," said Sarah.

"Has anyone made any funeral arrangements?" asked Bridget.

"Charles was the one who drafted Harvey's will, and I believe he said that Harvey had made arrangements for his funeral ahead of time. I think it's all paid for and planned with the funeral home in town. His body certainly won't be released for a while. He was murdered after all, and he will have an autopsy and things will have to be investigated before his body can be released. I'm sure that since Charles found the body and was Harvey's attorney, he will be informed of what is happening and I will let you know as soon as I know."

"I wonder if Anna has heard the news," said Sarah.

"I thought of calling her, but then we thought she should have her honeymoon to herself without worrying about something like this," said Fiona. "There's certainly nothing they can do for Harvey, and they deserve this time together, just the three of them."

They finished their lunch talking about things that were happening in their lives other than murder and split at the door to the restaurant. Sarah had to walk to the Braunleaven offices down the street and Bridget had driven her car to the hotel, but parked in a lot a few blocks away. So they said good-bye and vowed to let one another know if they thought of anything they could use to solve this puzzle.

The rest of Fiona's day was spent at home doing some mowing and cleaning around the front flower beds. She finished in time to take care of the horses for the night, shower and change into shorts and a tee-shirt, and heat up some left-over lasagna for dinner. When Charles came home from work he had his favorite meal again. He always liked it better the second time anyway, and it was a comfort after the busy day of meetings and dealing with the death of Harvey Glavin.

They each talked about how the day had gone over dinner, and while they cleaned the kitchen together, they discussed the arrangements that Harvey had made for himself. "His body is to be cremated, and then there is to be a wake at the funeral home," said

Charles. "The burial service must be held on a Sunday, and he would like someone to carry his ashes on the ride. I think we should all take turns. It's a nice tribute when you think about it. Harvey lived for the Sunday ride and in a way he'll be taking his last one. He left instructions for me to spread the ashes in the small cemetery on the grounds of the estate."

"Do you know when all of this will take place? Will his body be released soon?"

"I will call Garda Simms tomorrow and see about that. They may want to keep the body until they have an idea of who killed him, especially since he wanted to be cremated. Once that's done it makes finding any new evidence a bit difficult."

Just as they were about to turn in for the night, someone rang the doorbell and Charles went to answer it. The man standing on the top step looked familiar, but he couldn't place him. "Hello. My name is Andrew Glavin. I'm here about my brother."

That explained the familiarity. There was a definite family resemblance, although Andrew was clearly several years younger than Harvey had been, and much better looking. While Harvey had definitely let himself go in recent years, his brother was fit and healthy in appearance. Charles said, "Please come in."

"I'm sorry to bother you at home," he said stopping just inside the door. "I know you were Harvey's attorney, but you were also his friend. I've come for the key to my house."

"I'm sorry?"

"I need a place to stay while I'm here. I know that I'm to inherit his estate so I would like the keys so I don't have to break in."

"I don't have the key and I am certain that the house is still a crime scene. You will have to clear it with the local garda before you can be allowed in."

"Where do I find the garda station?"

"It's on the high street in town next to the bridge. You can't miss it."

Andrew turned and left the house after a slight smile and nod to Charles and Fiona. At that same moment the phone rang and Fiona answered. She handed the phone to Charles and told him that it was Garda Simms on the phone. "I wanted to let you know that we can now release the body to the funeral home. We've not found anything but the knife wound that is clearly the cause of death. He was in good health otherwise for his age. Whoever killed him left no evidence behind on the body."

"Okay. Thanks for the call. You might like to know that Harvey's brother was just here. He wanted me to give him the key to Harvey's house. I sent him to you and told him I thought the house might still be a crime scene."

"It is. He's going to have to find a different place to stay for a while, because he can't stay there."

"He also needs to know that he can't arrange to have Harvey's body released to him even though he is the only surviving relative. Harvey made and paid for his funeral arrangements in advance, so if this guy wants to save money on the funeral, he has no right to make changes."

"I won't offer any information at this time. I won't even tell him that we're done with the body unless he asks me directly. I certainly can't lie, but I don't have to be the one to bring it up. We don't know much about him and for all we know, he might be a suspect. My only conversation this night will be about the fact that he can't take possession of the house yet. He may argue, but if we find him in there before the house is cleared, we'll have to arrest him."

"Just so you know, he doesn't seem to be the friendliest fellow."

"Thanks for the heads up."

"I'll notify the funeral home director in the morning that he's to get the body. I'm also going to stop by sometime around noon tomorrow to show you the paperwork that he filled out about his arrangements, if that's alright with you."

"Sure. I'll see you then."

"Did you hear all of that?" he asked Fiona.

"I did. Andrew seems a bit odd. Do you think he's going to interfere with Harvey's wishes? It doesn't seem like he's mourning the way a brother should. His only concern seems to be where he's going to stay, not what happened to Harvey."

"I don't know, Fi. I have a feeling that this is going to get stranger before it gets straightened out. Let's go to bed. It's been a long day."

They turned the dogs out into the run for a short time while they locked the house and when they heard the dogs at the back door, they let them in and headed upstairs to turn in.

7

The Walkers got up early Wednesday morning so they could share breakfast before Charles went off to the office. He kissed Fiona good-bye and drove off with a wave out the car window. Fiona had horses to tend to and so when the breakfast dishes were finished she left for the stable. Just as she was finishing her chores a car drove into the stable courtyard. It was Bridget's BMW. She got out and said, "I have nothing on my schedule and I wondered if you'd like to go for a ride."

"In the car or on a horse?"

"Horse, please."

"Great. I'd love to."

Fiona and Charles came late to horseback riding. They never rode as kids since they were both from families that couldn't afford such an expensive sport. After they started dating they wanted to do some sort of physical activity together and they chose riding over their other options. They took lessons together and both of them loved it. It was one of the reasons that they bought the property they did. They enlisted the help of their riding instructor when they went shopping for horses and the result was a beautiful pair of Thoroughbred geldings of the same color and size. More importantly, they were both well trained and had quiet and dependable dispositions. They rode them for several years, but they had had some age on them when they bought them and the sometimes challenging Sunday rides became too difficult for them. The result was that they retired the pair and vowed that they would have a home for the rest of their lives. They could be ridden still, but not for long rides like the ones they took on Sundays. They went looking for another pair of Thoroughbreds, and because their riding skills had improved, they settled on a younger pair with a bit more energy and cross country ability.

The first two horses were visibly jealous whenever the other two were taken out and loaded into the trailer, so when the ride was short and not very challenging, the older pair was taken out, brushed to a shine and saddled up. Their attitudes changed from pasture lazy to heads up, tails high in the air and ready to go. Fiona and Bridget were going to ride them for about an hour on a loose rein over flat ground. It was enough exercise for them and they were glad to be selected for the ride, so off they went, and since the two women were not planning to leave Fiona's property, they allowed the dogs to join them. When they returned to the stable the older horses were happy to get back to their oats and hay.

It was a nice leisurely ride spent talking about their memories of Harvey Glavin. After the horses had been taken care of and returned to the pasture, Bridget and Fiona took Bridget's car back to the house for a lunch of ham and cheese sandwiches and a green salad. Fiona made a pitcher of lemonade and finished the meal with chocolate biscuits.

"We have to do this more often," said Fiona. "It reminds me of the days when we shared a flat and would have the rare day off together. We'd go to the pub down the street for lunch or get some take-out and eat on our tiny balcony. I miss that."

"I agree, but it has to be a day when Daniel is gone. He's gotten so annoying about wanting to know where I go and with whom. I can't do anything without reporting in. He's always questioning me as if he thinks I'm doing something I shouldn't. I sometimes think he wants to catch me doing something wrong. But I'm not supposed to question him about anything. Today he's gone to Galway on business, so I have a respite."

"Bridge, I can't tell you what to do about your own marriage, but it seems that every time I talk to you lately things have gotten worse with him. Why don't you see a counselor?"

"Believe it or not, I have actually suggested that to him. He won't hear of it. The last time I mentioned it he yelled at me and said not to ever bring that idea up again. He used to be such a fun person, remember? His personality has changed so much in the last year or so, it's as if he's a different man entirely. I'm close to leaving him. The problem is that we've sold everything except the two cars and the house, which is heavily mortgaged, to cover some bad business decisions. We have no assets to split and if I leave him I will have to go back to work. Even though I've kept my hand in by doing some volunteering, I've been out of nursing for so long I don't know if anyone will hire me. I also don't know if I can stand on my feet all day long anymore. Believe me, I've thought about it."

"You have three friends who will help you. I'll bet that if you asked Sarah, she would have a place where you could live for free. She has plenty of space in that huge house of hers, and she also has that beautiful guest house sitting there empty. If not you could stay with us until you find a place or Anna would make you the same offer. She even has an apartment over the garage, remember? Don't stay in an unhappy marriage because you have no place to go, because that's not true."

"Thanks. It means a lot to me that you're willing to help. I still want to try to make things work, but I'll keep all this in mind. Maybe I'm just too stubborn to give up, or maybe I'm just afraid of being on my own."

"I know what you mean, but look at Anna. She was left by Carl and now her life is better than it ever was and she thought she had been happy before. And Sarah is the same way, much better off out of a bad marriage."

"Just give me some time to think about it. It's good to know that I have friends to talk to. I promise that if it gets to the point that I can't take it anymore, I may show up on your doorstep."

"I hate to even hear you talk like that. Don't stay in an unhappy place. You deserve better than that."

"There's something I haven't told you yet. I have been sensing something going on with Daniel for some time now and I have been preparing for the worst."

"What do you mean by that?"

"I have been putting money aside for a while now. It isn't a lot at this point, but it is enough to tide me over for a while until I can figure out what I will do for the rest of my life."

"Are you serious?"

"I have a bank account in my own name that Daniel doesn't know about. It's enough so I can find an apartment and pay a few months' rent, and not a lot more than that. We have enough furniture in that big house that if we divide it between us I won't have to buy any. My car is paid for and it is in my name, so I would be able to take it with me."

"I guess this is serious. If you have made this kind of provision for the future, then it doesn't seem like you intend to fight for your marriage."

"I was willing to but he isn't, so no, I guess I don't. I truly do believe it's over, or it will be soon."

When Bridget left, Fiona walked with the dogs around the yard slowly, thinking about her best friend being so sad. She thought about the time when they had shared an apartment as young, single, working girls. Bridget had been so full of fun. She had the most infectious laugh. Now she could hardly get her to crack a smile. Harvey is dead, Bridget is unhappy, Anna is gone. What's going to happen next?

She spent the rest of the afternoon reading a book until time to fix dinner. Her sandwiches and salad at lunch had been so enjoyable that she planned the same thing for dinner with the addition of a bowl of thick soup. When he got home Charles changed his clothes and they took their dinner out to the gazebo in the yard with a bottle of Braunleaven wine from Sarah's vineyard. Fiona filled him in on the problems Bridget was having and he agreed with her that Bridget should take care of herself. He said, "With no kids to worry about she should cut her losses and not wonder about what she would do for a living. I like Daniel, but we have no idea what goes on behind closed doors. If he's making her this unhappy she should leave him."

Just as they were finishing their meal, a strange car drove into the yard and a large man got out and walked toward them. Charles had to call back the dogs who had gone to see who dared to come into their yard. When he got to the gazebo, he held out his hand to shake and said, "Hello. My name is Phil Waters. I worked as Harvey Glavin's gamekeeper for many years. I'm here because I heard that he was dead. Is that true?"

"Yes, I'm sorry, but that is true."

"Oh, don't be sorry. I'm not. He was an ungrateful bastard, and more than that in my opinion. I'm here because I'm thinking I might have been mentioned in his will. I understand you are his attorney."

"I am, and I would be glad to talk to you in my office in the morning, although I'm not sure how much I can tell you at this time."

"I understand. Would it be alright if I were to go to your office at 9:00 in the morning?"

"That'll be fine, but there are things to be done before his estate can be made public. He was murdered, after all."

"Fine. I understand that. But I'll be there anyway. If I am in the will, I have rights." With that he turned and stomped back to his car and drove away.

"Okay. This is the second night in a row that we've had an unwelcome visitor. Should we move to the Gentry until this is settled?"

They took their dishes back to the house as it was becoming dark and after they finished in the kitchen and took care of the animals, they turned in early again.

8

Fiona woke early on Thursday to share breakfast with Charles before he left for the office, after which she cleaned the kitchen of the breakfast mess and took the two dogs with her to the stable to take care of the horses. She paid particular attention to Harvey's horse and had the feeling that he was beginning to feel at home. As she was trying to decide whether to go back to the house or take a horseback ride, Sarah pulled into the courtyard in her Mini Cooper. Fiona's first words to her were, "I want to go for a ride, but I don't want to go alone. Do you have time?"

"I do and I'd love to go. Can I ride Harvey's horse? I've always wanted to try him out, but I never dared to ask Harvey."

"That would be good. If we ride him with one of our horses they can become familiar with each other and that will make it easier to introduce Big Tim into the pasture."

"Good. Isn't it lucky that I travel with a pair of riding boots in my car?" With that, Sarah changed into her boots and they went to saddle Big Tim and Anna's horse for a ride.

They rode only on Fiona's property so that the dogs could run along behind the horses, with occasional forays into the woods to hunt for critters. "What would happen if they ever found a wild animal to chase?" asked Sarah.

"If either of them ever found a wild animal they would run for the hills, but they put on a good show, don't they?"

"They do. I came here to talk to you about the note that Harvey left on his desk. There was something about it that I didn't think about at lunch the other day. Do you remember that the note said that the papers were 'down under in the desk'?"

"Yes."

"Big Tim doesn't have papers."

"What?"

"Henry told me all about Big Tim. He bought a mare from a friend of his and he didn't realize at the time that the mare was with foal. In the meantime, the man who sold him the mare died. The foal was born and Henry had no way of getting papers on him, but he really liked him. So he had him trained and had planned to keep him for himself as a Sunday horse. Then Harvey's old horse died and Henry knew that he couldn't afford another quality horse, so he gave him Big Tim. So that makes me wonder why Harvey would say where to find the papers when there are no papers."

"Interesting. Then that makes me feel even more certain that that note was a puzzle after all. I wonder what 'down under in the drawer' means. I think that making the note seem like a will was probably just to fool the killer into letting him leave the note, but 'down under in the drawer' is just not the way people talk. I think we need to get a look at that desk. Charles and I have a small house and it is completely furnished. The desk that we have in the office is one that we found in an antique shop and refinished ourselves. We are both really proud of it and Harvey knew that. Leaving that huge desk to Charles is a clue, too. I'm sure of it. And he said to tell Charles that his will was with his lawyer. Charles was his lawyer. I'd love to get in and look 'down under' in that desk to see what he might have meant."

"We can't get to the desk. The house is still a crime scene."

"I know. We are going to have to give this some thought."

"No, Fiona. We should tell Garda Simms and let him figure it out. Whoever killed Harvey could still be around and I for one don't want to risk meeting up with a murderer."

"You're right, of course. I'll tell Charles and he can pass the information along to Simms. On another subject, I think Bridget is getting ready to leave Daniel."

"To be honest, I'm not really surprised. I think there has been trouble there for a long time. I am going to go so far as to say that I'm glad that she's going to leave him. I've been in a bad marriage and leaving it was the best thing I ever did. Of course, I didn't really leave it; the Jackass did. But you know what I mean." Sarah's first husband had been named Jack, hence the nickname. He had left her for a younger woman who had since left him. He had made contact with her and had threatened to get money out of her one way or another. His threats had been met with the guarantee that her security force was up to his challenge, and she hadn't heard from him since. "I, like Anna, am living proof that leaving a marriage is not only not always the end of the world; it's sometimes the best thing that can happen."

"I agree, but getting to that point is not going to be easy for her. There is going to be a problem with money. I opened my mouth and suggested that you might offer her your guest house."

"Of course. I can have it ready in a matter of hours. That way she could be around friends but still have a place to be alone."

As they returned to the stable Fiona said, "If I talk to her before you do I'll tell her that, if it's okay with you."

"It's certainly okay with me." They unsaddled the horses, gave them each a quick sponge bath and rub down, and put them in the pasture. As Sarah got in her car to leave, she said, "Let me know if you hear anything about either Bridget or Harvey's note."

"Will do. Bye my friend."

Sarah went home and Fiona went to her house trailing two tired dogs behind her. The rest of Fiona's day was divided between light housework and giving the two dogs a good brushing. During their run in the woods they had collected many twigs and burs in their coats and she pulled and combed until they were sleek and tangle free. When Charles called from work and said he would pick up Chinese food on the way home, she was delighted. They ate outside in the gazebo and then went to take care of the horses together. Fiona told him about the news she had gotten from Sarah about the horse's papers and he was puzzled. "That makes no sense," he said.

"It does if he was trying to tell you something. What better way to draw your attention to a clue he was leaving than to write something that didn't make sense? You see how we're talking and thinking about it; I think that is just what he wanted us to do. What about the game keeper who came here last night? Did he go to your office this morning?"

"Yes. He showed up and wanted to know about Harvey's will. He wanted to know who would inherit and what Harvey's principal heir planned to do with the place. I told him that a will was private and that I could not discuss it with him. I said the will would be read after the investigation into his murder was finished and then he would find out all about anything that Harvey might have left him."

"Judging from his behavior here last night, I can't imagine that that made him very happy."

"No, it did not. He stormed out and left my office in a hurry.

He did say something odd before he left, though. He said he had gotten a letter from Harvey saying that he should come here to allow him to make amends."

"Did he say why they would need to make amends?"

"No. I couldn't get him to say much more."

"Things just seem to get stranger and stranger."

They dawdled in the barn enjoying the combination of physical labor and peace and quiet. They decided to try to introduce Big Tim to the rest of the horses. After a few squeals and harmless kicks, the five horses calmed down to the extent that Charles and Fiona felt confident that the five of them would be fine together. They moved him into one of the stalls that led to the pasture, and as darkness fell they dragged their tired bodies homeward.

9

Friday morning Fiona slept until almost 9:00. Charles left her a note on his pillow. "Hey Sleepy Head. I let you sleep, but I imagine there are some horses waiting for you. I let the dogs out before I left, so you shouldn't have any puddles to clean up. I also fed them. Have a good day and I'll see you tonight."

Fiona jumped out of bed and dressed for the stables. When she got there she was met by nickering from horses who were accustomed to an earlier breakfast. "I'm sorry guys. I won't let it happen again." She gave them all some oats and then opened their outside doors to let them go out to pasture for the day and made their stalls ready for night with more oats and some hay, and checked their water buckets to make sure they were clean. She mucked their stalls and swept the floor and left the stable visitor ready. She was hungry herself and left in a hurry to get her own breakfast. No matter how hungry she was, when she slept in late, the animals needed to be fed first.

When she got to the kitchen her weekly housekeeper was there cleaning already and laundry was being done. This was Fiona's cue to get out of the house. She grabbed a yogurt and called Bridget to set up a time for lunch. The two of them met at Kelley's Pub at 12:00. They often went to Kerrigan's, but it was a popular place for tourists. The pub front was clean and freshly painted in bright colors and it was a magnet for crowds. Bridget and Fiona liked Kelley's because the façade showed wear and the sign needed repainting, but it was left that way on purpose. It was a small, family-owned pub that catered to locals. They served the best Irish stew in town, but Bridget and Fiona settled for salads with grilled chicken and hot rolls. They placed their order as they walked in and found a table in the back corner where they could eat in peace.

"I had a ride with Sarah yesterday," said Fiona. "I told her about your problems with Daniel and she said she would be able to have her guest house ready for you to move in, in a matter of hours. And she really wants you to do it if you and Daniel split. But you knew she would make that offer, of course."

"She's wonderful. I knew she would and I really appreciate

it. Things didn't go well last night. I tried to get him to talk, but he was having none of it. There's constant tension. I don't know how much more I can take if things don't change."

"I'm sorry. I hate that things are going badly for you."

"Thanks for the concern, but right now my marriage is the last thing I want to talk about. I'm here to forget about it for a while. Is there anything new on the Harvey Glavin front?"

Fiona told her about what Sarah had said about the fact that there were no papers on Harvey's horse, and what Charles had said about the gamekeeper and Harvey making amends. "I wish we could find out something about Harvey. We really didn't know him that well. He was pretty private."

"Oh, my God!" said Bridget.

"What?"

"I can't believe that I forgot this. My grandmother used to work for Harvey."

"You're kidding. Can we talk to her?"

"If you take her lemon bars, she'll talk for hours. She lives at St. Gerald's."

"Isn't that where Sarah's friend Braden Ahern lived?"

"It is. We could go to the bakery on the high street and get her some lemon bars and then drive out to see her."

They ate their lunch and made the quick side-trip to the bakery and then went to see Bridget's grandmother. They drove up the long driveway and circled around in front of the imposing building that was once a private mansion, and was now repurposed as a home for the elderly, where they were pampered and lived their final days in comfort. They parked in the visitor lot and walked up to and through the front doors. The desk was unattended, but Bridget knew where her Gran would be on a beautiful day like this one. She was in the garden when they walked out the glass doors and she perked up when she saw Bridget. She remained seated but squeezed her granddaughter's hand and Bridget leaned over to hug her. She had met Fiona several times, but she had not seen her for a while. They exchanged greetings and Bridget presented her with the treats they had brought. They all took one and announced them delicious.

"Gran, did you hear that Harvey Glavin died?"

"No, I didn't. When did that happen?"

"He was found on Sunday night, but it's possible that he died as early as Friday afternoon."

"That's too bad. Did he have a fall or a heart attack?"

"This is something that you can't talk about. Do you promise?"

"You know I can't do a lot of things that I used to be able to do, but I can still keep a secret. Why all the mystery?"

"Harvey was killed. He was in his home by himself and someone broke in and stabbed him to death."

"Murdered?"

"Yes, Gran. You worked for him, didn't you?"

"I did, for several years."

"What can you tell us about him?"

A voice from behind them said, "Are you friends of Sarah Braunlea?"

They turned and both saw a handsome middle-aged woman staring at them with arms akimbo. They both responded to her at the same time, "Yes, we are." Bridget's grandmother introduced her and Fiona to Sandy, the matron and guardian at St. Gerald's.

"Now don't you even think about involving your grandmother in a murder investigation like Sarah did with Braden Ahern," she said sternly. She liked Sarah and she knew that Mr. Ahern had had the time of his life bringing a killer to justice at an age when he thought there was going to be no more excitement in his life, but she was not going to allow that to happen again.

"No," said Bridget. "I promise I would never do that to my grandmother. We were just talking to her about the time she spent working for Harvey Glavin. He died recently."

"Okay, but you had better keep your word. As long as that's all you're doing then I would gladly send some tea out for the three of you to have with your lemon bars. You know your grandmother well. She loves her lemon bars." Sandy walked back to the building and entered through the glass door. Shortly afterward, a young woman brought a tray with tea, cups, lemon, milk and sugar. She asked how everyone took their tea and prepared it for them. She handed around the cups and saucers, asked if she could do anything else for the three of them, and then returned to the building.

10

Bridget's gran started her story about the time, many years ago, when she started working as a scullery maid in the main house on Harvey's estate. "I got the job as soon as I left school. My family didn't have much and the job provided me a place to live along with the salary. I didn't make a lot of money, but I was given a uniform and all my meals. The days were long but I was young and strong and I knew that I had an advantage over many people my age who had to do hard physical labor. Some of the boys I knew had to work in the mines and some of the girls did factory work. The worst thing I had to do was scrub floors which I would have had to do if I had my own place to live, so I didn't mind it. I had several good friends there and on our days off we could get a ride into town and buy sweets and go on picnics. We shared a large room and often sat up nights talking and laughing. It wasn't a bad time of my life. In fact, I would say I had a lot of fun while I was there. I worked there for several years and that's where I met your grandfather. I worked inside the house and he was in charge of the horse breeding for Harvey. Your mother was born while we worked there and shortly after that we left when your grandfather and his brother went into business together."

"What kind of person was Harvey? What was he like to work for?"

"He was alright to me. He didn't pay any attention to those of us who worked when everyone was out of the room. We were supposed to be invisible and as far as he was concerned we certainly were." She leaned toward the two younger women and whispered as if she were telling a secret. "That meant that he would say things as if we weren't in the room. So I heard a lot that I'm sure he didn't want me to hear."

"Like what?"

"He talked a lot about the people who hadn't paid him the proper amount of respect and how he would get even with them. He talked about how he had the garda in his pocket, so if he wanted to do something that wasn't quite legal, he didn't have to worry about any repercussions. One time he was talking to some of his, we called them 'strong-arm men' among the house staff, about whether or not they had taken care of that little problem he had given them. One of them replied that he wasn't to worry. 'He won't be coming back.' Mr. Glavin noticed me cleaning the fireplace at that point and yelled at me to get out, and if I knew what was good for me I wouldn't repeat anything I had just heard. Of course I didn't. I had no idea what they were talking about anyway, and I didn't want to lose my job, or worse."

Bridget and Fiona realized that Gran wanted to share other secrets, so they leaned toward her and with their eyes opened wide and a shared smile, they asked her what she could tell them about his brother.

"He didn't get along with his brother. The entire estate was left to Harvey as was the custom in those days, and as soon as their father died Harvey told him he had to get out. Harvey's attorneys said he couldn't do that because his brother wasn't old enough. So Harvey waited and when his brother was of age, Harvey told him to take what he could fit into his bags, go to the bank and get his trust fund, and leave. They had a huge fight about that. There were threats on both sides. The brother said he would get even with Harvey someday, and Harvey said that if he ever stepped foot on the estate again he would shoot him. There was talk that he thought his young wife might have taken to Andrew instead of him. Of course, he always thought everyone was out to get him."

"Was there anything between the brother and the wife?"

"I never saw any evidence of it."

"Did the brother ever come back?" asked Fiona.

"Not that I know of. Then there was that young man who was in love with Harvey's wife before they got married. He showed up one night and pushed his way into the house and said he wanted to see her and Harvey yelled at him something awful. He had him taken away in a wagon. I saw him in the back of it and it looked as if he had taken quite a beating. We never saw him around there again, either."

"Did you know his name?" asked Bridget.

"No, but a maid in the house said Mrs. Glavin was watching out the window when they drove him away and she was crying hard. The story was that she and this man had been planning to get married as soon as she came of age. Before that she would need her father's permission and he had no intention of giving it to her. About a month before her birthday, he told her she was going to marry Harvey Glavin. Harvey had given him a piece of land he had been trying to buy from Lord Glavin for years. It was a trade for his daughter."

"Harvey's father was a lord?" asked Fiona.

"No, he just acted like he was so much better than everybody else that we called him Lord Glavin, not to his face of course."

"So this woman was basically sold to Harvey."

"It happened that way back then with people with money. Daughters weren't worth much to them except as bargaining chips. So Harvey married her and she never got to see her beau again. She told her maid that there was no way he would leave her there if he were still alive. She thought Harvey had had him killed and she was distraught about it."

"That must have been horrible for her," said Bridget. "I'm sure that must have made her hate Harvey, but what kind of marriage was it before that happened?"

"It was no kind of marriage I wanted. He bossed her around something terrible. He told her what books she could read, what clothes she could wear, where she could or couldn't go, who she could talk to, which wasn't very many people. One night they had a party and she went down the stairs wearing a lovely gown, and right in front of all their guests, Mr. Glavin told her to go back upstairs and take off that hideous dress. She did it, but it humiliated her."

"That poor woman."

Fiona asked, "Do you remember a gamekeeper who was let go after many years?"

"Oh yes. That was terrible. Gamekeeper was a responsible and prestigious position back in those days. His father had worked in that job for Lord Glavin. So when the fathers died the sons took over. The two of them had been close, and Harvey's father had even seen to it that Phil, that was the son of the old gamekeeper, got a decent education. Everything between the two of them seemed to be good until Mr. Glavin married. The Mrs. was so unhappy, but she did go out each day for a walk. They were short walks at first, but I think she realized that the longer she walked, the more time she could spend away from her husband." Again she leaned in as if to tell a secret. "There was a rumor that the gamekeeper and Mrs. Glavin would meet in the woods when Mr. Glavin was gone."

"Sounds like *Lady Chatterley's Lover*," said Fiona.

"No, it wasn't like that. He was a nice man and when Mrs. Glavin would go for a walk he would meet up with her. She even asked her maid to help with a tryst one time; that's how I knew what was going on. It was all hush-hush, and no one wanted to tell Mr. Glavin because they all saw how he treated her, but he found out somehow."

"What happened?" asked Bridget.

"None of us working inside the house knew at the time how he found out, but one day he called the gamekeeper into his study and fired him. He told him he had one hour to get his belongings and get off his property. He said that if he set foot on the estate again, he would be shot, just like he told his brother. Mr. Glavin's men took him to his cottage and watched him pack and then took him off, too. That poor woman was at her wit's end. She probably felt that she had no one left to turn to. I guess that's why she did what she did."

Together both women asked, "What did she do?"

"Why, they say she killed herself."

"She did?"

"That's the story."

"How did she do it?"

"She supposedly cut her wrists with Lord Glavin's letter opener."

Bridget and Fiona looked at each other in shock. Why had they never heard of this?

"What do you mean, supposedly?" asked Fiona.

"I never really believed it."

"Why not?"

"She used me as her personal maid one weekend when her regular maid had to go home because of a death in the family. I was in her room several times. Every time I walked in she was on her knees praying. She had a crucifix on the wall over her bed and she read from the Bible every night before she retired. She was a devout Catholic. Mr. Glavin would never allow her to go to church, but she kept her religion as much as she could. In her faith, suicide is a mortal sin. If a person commits suicide they can't go to heaven; they couldn't even be buried in a Catholic cemetery in those days. I don't believe she would ever do anything like that."

Bridget looked deep into her grandmother's eyes. "Are you saying that you think she was murdered?"

"I can't think of any other explanation. Besides, Mr. Glavin never allowed her to go into his study. He said that the only women allowed in his study were the maids who waited on him. So how would she have gotten that letter opener? It was always on his desk in the study. I don't even see how she would know he had it."

"Was it ever investigated as a possible murder?"

"No. You have to understand that in those days Mr. Glavin was very influential. He could make things like that go away. That's why nothing ever came of him beating that other man the way he did. No one dared to cross him."

Bridget turned to Fiona and said, "We need to find out more about these people. Any one of them could have wanted to kill Harvey."

"Gran, thank you for the information. You are amazing. You have given us so much to work with. Thank you so much," said Bridget as she got up to leave.

"You are most definitely welcome. If you have any more questions, I'd love to help." Gran's voice lowered and her face became drawn. "I have often felt that if I had done something, or said something about what was going on in that house, that Mrs. Glavin might not have died the way she did."

"Gran, you couldn't have stopped him. You were a young girl and he was rich and powerful. If you had said something, you might have suffered a similar fate."

"Still, I can't help but…Anyway, you and your friend here should come and visit me more often."

"And bring lemon bars?"

"Oh, I wouldn't mind."

11

Bridget had driven from the pub to St. Gerald's, so after the visit to her Gran she drove Fiona back to the pub to get her car. By the time Fiona got home and fixed and put a casserole in the oven for dinner, Charles was driving in the driveway. He walked into the house and found her in the kitchen. "How was your day?" he asked her as he put his arms around her waist.

"I had a good day and I have a lot to tell you. How about you?"

"I had a good day, too, and when I get my clothes changed, you and I can go to the stable and take care of our herd," he said with a chuckle. "While we are working we can talk about our respective news. Agreed?"

"Agreed."

Charles went upstairs and changed his clothes, and when he came down he and Fiona left for the barn. "Tell me about your news," Fiona said as they walked.

"Well, most of my day was absolutely not newsworthy. Then about 3:00 this afternoon I had a visit from Harvey's brother Andrew. He is anxious to get into Harvey's house and the police aren't letting him near the place. I asked him what he had in mind for the house and he said he plans to tear it down. He wants to auction off all of the contents. He feels that he can make a lot of money by selling everything piecemeal and then he can sell the land for development. I asked him if he had any attachment to the house or the contents at all and he said no. He said that he wouldn't live in the place if the alternative were to be homeless."

"He sounds charming."

"The house is a disaster. In order to live in it he would have to spend a fortune on renovation. I wouldn't live in it either if I were he. Anyway, I kind of like the guy. I gather that his family life left a lot to be desired. He and Harvey were really close when they were young, but they didn't get along at all after their mother died and their father was always distant and unavailable to him. He gave all of his attention to Harvey as the heir to the estate, and Harvey began to feel naturally superior to him. When his father died he left Andrew nothing from the estate except for a small trust fund. His father was one of those still hanging on to the practice of primogeniture. Harvey could have let him stay on the property at least, but he threw him out. That's not a way to promote brotherly love," he said as they approached the first stall where Big Tim was waiting to come in to eat.

"I heard the same thing today and that Harvey thought the brother was a threat to his marriage. I also heard that Harvey told him that if he stepped foot on the property again he would shoot him," said Fiona as she opened the door and let the horse in.

"Whoa, where did you get that information?"

"It turns out that Bridget's grandmother used to work for Harvey. We went to see her today and she told us all about Harvey and the kind of man he used to be. It seems that the Harvey we knew, and thought was just a kind old man who had fallen on hard times, was actually a total tyrant. He used his money and his position to push people around, sometimes with violence. I'm liking him less and less as I get to know about him."

Charles let the two old horses into their stalls and took a seat on a tack box and said, "Tell me what you learned."

She continued with the two remaining horses as she told Charles about what they had heard from Bridget's Gran, the most shocking part of it being the fact that Gran didn't believe that Harvey's wife had committed suicide. "She was supposed to have killed herself with Harvey's letter opener, but Bridget's Gran didn't even think she would have known where it was."

"That's interesting. There's pretty strong evidence that Harvey was killed with that same letter opener. And whoever killed him took the opener with him."

Fiona finished her report about the same time that they finished their work. They returned to the house and after cleaning up, they put the dinner on the table and dined on potato and chicken casserole. It was peasant food and they enjoyed it along with a salad and a glass of wine that made the meal seem more impressive.

"How are the plans for the funeral coming along?" she asked him as she took a forkful of salad.

"As you know, everything was planned in advance. The body has been collected by the funeral home, and as far as I know, it will be cremated soon if it has not been already. And services won't be ready for tomorrow, so I would say that the wake will be some day next week and we'll spread the ashes on Sunday next."

"Wouldn't it be more convenient for you to wait until Saturday for the wake?"

"Yes. I am leaning that way if it's alright with you."

"You're the one with a job outside the home. Any day is fine with me."

"Then I'll call tomorrow and set that date. We'll put it in the paper to let people know." When dinner was done they performed the nightly routines including cleaning the kitchen and letting out the dogs. Then they opted for an early night with a movie on the television. They both fell asleep before it ended as a result of a busy day.

12

Saturday was Charles' day off, and unlike many attorneys, he did not allow his work to change that. He dealt with legal issues that involved finances, inheritances, property settlements, and other matters that didn't normally need to be decided on an emergency basis. He felt that his time on Saturdays was important to him and to Fiona, and the Sunday ride was sacrosanct. Some clients felt that their problems required their attorneys to cater to them on weekends, evenings and holidays, and Charles simply told them that they should find someone else to represent them. It was a testament to his value to the firm that he was allowed by the other partners to do so. And it was a testament to his reputation as one of the best lawyers in the city that people were willing to wait for him when they would not have waited for a lesser attorney.

This Saturday, after the barn chores were finished, was a day to do some yard work including tree pruning and shrub trimming, not the major work that was reserved for a real landscaper, but the smaller plants. They did the work together as they did almost everything. The work was hard and the yard was large, so the day was spent by the time they finished. They stopped twice to eat and once more to take care of their animals, and after they showered and dressed for bed they succumbed to exhaustion.

When they woke Sunday morning they were ready for the ride of the week. They trailered to the home of Sam and June Chambers who lived over twenty miles away. They were among the farthest afield for most of the riders. This gave them the opportunity to ride lands that they only saw twice a year. The weather wasn't clear and comfortable. There was an unseasonable chill in the air and the attire was windbreakers over their polo shirts. But the breakfast was tasty and the champagne was as well, and off they went hoping the rain would wait until the ride ended.

Bridget and Fiona waited for Sarah to catch up to them before falling in behind the others. "Sorry. I was chatting and didn't notice when the ride began. So, Bridget, tell me how things are going for you and Daniel."

"I think it's just a matter of time until we split. I have tried to ignore some things, but lately I have begun to think he's cheating on me and I also think that I have to call it quits. Every night I sit there, often on my own, and I think, 'Is this the way it's supposed to be?' And the answer is no. I would rather be alone and single than alone and married to someone who is off with somebody else. On the other hand, I don't want to rush into something and not give him the benefit of the doubt. Maybe tonight, after the ride, we can have a talk. I just haven't been able to get any time alone with him."

"Just remember that if you do decide to make the move, you have friends to help you."

"Thanks for that. Let's talk about something else. Did Fiona tell you about our visit to my Gran yesterday?"

"No. You both went to St. Gerald's? I haven't been there since Braden's memorial."

"Yes. And Sandy wanted to make sure we weren't getting my Gran involved in a murder mystery the way you did with Braden Ahern."

The three of them shared a laugh as they remembered how upset Sandy had been with Sarah, even though she knew she had been a dear friend to her former charge.

"You see, I remembered something that I certainly would have remembered earlier if I hadn't had other things on my mind. My grandmother worked for Harvey Glavin when she was just out of school. She had some interesting things to say about our dear friend Harvey." Between the two of them, Bridget and Fiona filled Sarah in on what Gran had said. She also was as shocked as Charles had been at the suggestion that Harvey's wife's death was not a suicide after all.

"Speaking of things we should have remembered, I should consult the journals." Sarah was referring to the Braunlea journals that had been kept by all the heirs of her estate, Braunleaven. They started with the Henry who built the house and continued through each generation. In fact, writing them was one of the jobs that she had taken on when her husband died. They were a version of local history from the point of view of the writer and had contained useful information about the mystery of a murder that had taken place near Sarah's estate over thirty years earlier. "When I get home tonight I will see what I can find out about the Glavins. I read the journals already, but it was before I knew anything about Harvey. I didn't pay particular attention to what was written about him. I was reading the journals to Henry for a distraction after he was confined to his bed and I was paying more attention to him than to what I was reading. The other thing is that some of my former husband's ancestors had different ideas about what was right and what was wrong. Surely any of them would have felt that Harvey had every right to treat his wife like chattel."

"We should have lunch and you can tell us what you found. How about tomorrow at that new place that we have been wanting to try north of town? I think it's called the Blue Swan. We could meet at 1:00."

The others agreed and the date was set. Fiona also told them about the time of the wake for Harvey and that next Sunday's ride would be the day that they would carry his ashes.

Charles and Fiona trailered their horses home and put them and the others in for the night. They walked to the house and were greeted by the dogs who went out for their evening constitutional while their owners had a quick sandwich for dinner. The late breakfast that they had eaten in the morning was long gone, but since Fiona rarely cooked after a ride and because they were going straight to bed, they ate light. Fiona told her husband about Sarah's plans to look for information about Harvey in her journals. They let in the dogs and headed upstairs. "I don't know how much you'll get from her journals. They are mostly about Braunleaven and what goes on there, but maybe there will be a bit of insight. I'll be interested in what she finds."

"Have you heard anything from Garda Simms lately?"

"Not really. That's something else I should do tomorrow when I get a chance. I should check in with him. I am certain though that the house is still a crime scene."

"Will you tell him about what Bridget's Gran said?"

"Yes, Dear."

"And about the horse not having papers?"

"Yes, Dear."

As they climbed into bed, she leaned over, kissed him on the cheek and said, "In the words of Scarlett O'Hara, 'Tomorrow is another day.' Good night."

13

Fiona's morning went as usual and she left home in time to reach the new restaurant by 1:00. It was an old stone house that had been purchased by a young couple fresh out of culinary school. It was two stories high and the upstairs had been made into office space and a private dining area. The food was carried to the upper floor by a dumbwaiter. The out-of-the-way seating was perfect for private parties or company meetings. They had converted the ground floor into an open plan with the kitchen in full view. They believed that people would enjoy seeing the food preparation process. It seemed that they were right because the place became popular immediately with the local foodies. On a Monday, though, it was possible to get a table for lunch right away without a reservation.

The three friends met outside the building and when they entered the restaurant they were ushered into the dark-wood paneled dining area downstairs and seated at a window table with a view of a small stream and a perfectly manicured lawn. There was a large stone fireplace with a wooden slab for a mantle. It looked as if it would be inviting on a winter evening. The tables were covered with light blue table cloths and set with Lennox china decorated with blue swans. It was a perfect combination of old and new.

"If the food is as good as the décor, it will be delightful," said Fiona.

They were approached by a young waitress and were given menus and glasses of ice water. They all selected the special, blackened salmon with rice pilaf and steamed asparagus, and chose a dry white wine. When the waitress left to place their order Sarah brought out her notes from her journals. "I copied passages to bring with me, because I got information from several different entries. Understand that the journal entries are usually short and concise. The Braunleas left the details to the newspapers. But I did find some interesting things."

The waitress brought some hot rolls and pickles to the table and Sarah waited until she had left to begin. "I have three entries that relate to Harvey and his brother. This first one is taken from the journal of Henry's grandfather. It has to do with Harvey's father. It tells us the sort of man those two boys had to live with."

> *Fergal Glavin rode over today to repay some of his debt. His wife died and he asked me about who he could get to take care of his son. I said he must mean his sons, not his son and he said the younger one didn't need anything in the way of education. He had done enough for him. He just needed to take care of the older one. He would inherit and so he was the only one that counted. I am considered to be a bit of a bastard, but even I don't think you just disregard one of your kids. After all, what if something happens to the older one and the younger one inherits? If he's paid no attention to the younger one he'll know nothing about running the estate.*

"I'm sorry, but these people were horrible. Fergal Glavin didn't care at all about his kids, only his estate. And Henry's grandfather doesn't seem to be much better."

"I told you the journals were full of this kind of thing. Henry was a bit embarrassed about the way his family lived their lives. But they were a product of their times, I guess."

At that point the lunch arrived and they each took a bite. They pronounced it among the best salmon they had ever eaten. It was fresh and spicy and went perfectly with the rice and vegetable. They all agreed that Anna was going to enjoy this new lunch spot. They were distracted from their conversation for a bit, but got back to it eventually. "The next entry was written by Henry's father. He was just as bad as his father had been, if not worse. Honestly, I don't know how Henry turned out as well as he did coming from people like these."

> *Harvey Glavin married his neighbor's daughter last week. There was no ceremony, just a minister at the house.*

> *The rumor is that he got her in exchange for a piece of land that her father had been wanting for a while. It wasn't that great a deal for Harvey. She has no money to contribute to the estate. He should have shopped around a bit. He isn't the businessman his father was and he'll probably lose everything his ancestors have worked for. What a fool he is.*

"Then he writes another entry just a couple of years later."

> *Harvey Glavin's wife died yesterday. The rumor is that she did herself in. I don't believe it, but it's none of my business. I knew from the start that he'd made a bad deal in marrying her. There'll be no funeral.*

"The last one comes from Henry's journal. I'm proud to say that I married the best of the Braunlea line."

> *Harvey Glavin paid me a visit today. His horse died and he doesn't have enough money for a new one. I told him he could have Big Tim. He's a good ride and I can't get much for him without papers. Harvey has an exalted view of himself, and I will never forget how badly he treated his wife, but he's an old man now and the only thing he enjoys these days is riding. So I'll give him Big Tim. I'm sure he'll take good care of him. If he doesn't I'll take him back.*

"You're right," said Fiona. "You did marry the best of the lot."

"So from this we can confirm that Harvey was treated much better than his brother which could make him want to get revenge on Harvey. We know that the story about his trading land for a wife is true, and that Big Tim had no papers. We also know that Harvey mistreated his wife. We already knew this, but we have written documentation of it now from what we would consider reliable sources who actually knew the people involved," said Bridget. "And we also have at least two people who believe that her death might not have been a suicide."

"I think we need to find out more about the brother, the gamekeeper, and the boyfriend who disappeared from the face of the earth," said Fiona. "We don't know if Harvey killed his wife. Even if we know that his wife wouldn't have killed herself, it doesn't mean that he did it. It's possible that one of our other suspects killed them both."

"If the gamekeeper and his father both worked for the Glavins, then we should be able to find out about them. The boyfriend grew up around here so we should be able to find out who he was, and as far as the brother is concerned, he was a member of a well-known family. He should be the easiest of the three."

"I don't want to be the constant wet blanket, but I really think this is a case for the gards. I don't want to get hurt and I certainly don't want either of you in danger either. I think it is fine to talk about this over lunch, but when it comes to investigating a possible murderer, we really need to leave this to Simms. He's good at what he does and if he encounters the killer he will be better prepared to deal with him than we would. I can't stress enough how unpleasant it is to be in fear for your life. And if Anna were here she would back me up."

The other two agreed that there was potential for danger and that they needed to allow the professionals to take care of it. They finished their meal and paid the waitress who took care of the payment herself. As they got ready to leave, Fiona asked to speak to the owner. She came from behind the kitchen counter and Fiona told her how much they had enjoyed their meal. The other two echoed her sentiments to the delight of the new owner. "We will let our friends know about how good the food is. And of course, we will be back ourselves." The owner, who introduced herself as Jane Lindley, was obviously pleased at the report.

The three friends got into their cars and left for their homes vowing to give thought to how they might learn more about the people in the case of who murdered Harvey Glavin without getting into trouble themselves.

14

That evening Charles got home from work early to find Fiona just getting ready to prepare dinner. He said, "Why don't we order a pizza tonight? I feel like pepperoni and cheese. We can wait until the horses are taken care of and eat a little later. What do you say?"

"That's fine with me. I'll put these things away while you change and we'll head for the barn."

He returned in a matter of minutes, and the two of them set off for the stable with the dogs trailing behind. They took their time doing the work and Fiona told him about their lunch. She first told him she had found their new dining spot, and then she told him that he had been right about Sarah's journals. There was information in them, but not very much and nothing they didn't know already. She did feel that some of their earlier information had been confirmed. They returned to the house and Charles called in the order for pizza.

When the doorbell rang he took the money from his pocket and opened the door. He was surprised to see not the pizza boy, but Bridget and she had been crying. He opened the door wide for her and she went in and stood in the foyer. "Is something wrong?" he asked, knowing that it was a stupid question.

Bridget forced a laugh and said, "Something is wrong and something is finally right."

Fiona came down the stairs and said, "Is it pizza?"

"No, it's Bridget and I think she needs a friend."

"Bridget. Does this mean what I think it means?"

"It does. I told him tonight that I couldn't take it anymore. All we do is fight on the rare occasions that we are both at home. I packed a few bags and put them in my car and drove right here. Sarah has a company thing tonight so I haven't let her know yet. Besides, it will take her some time to get the guest house ready. Will you let me stay here tonight?"

"Of course. Stay as long as you need." Fiona put her arm around Bridget's shoulder and led her into the kitchen where she was getting plates and glasses of wine ready for dinner. "We're just about to have pizza, so you've come just in time."

At that point the doorbell rang again. This time it was the delivery boy and Charles paid for dinner. He turned to the two women with the box in his hand and said, "Pizza anyone?"

No sooner had he gotten the pizza onto a platter and carried it to the table where the two women were already seated, than the doorbell rang again. "I'll get it," he said. He returned to the dining room followed by Brian Anderson, Shane's brother. "I think we're going to need another plate," he said. "I'm glad I ordered a large."

15

It was a pleasant meal and it seemed for a while to take their minds off Bridget's news. The four of them talked comfortably about the whereabouts of the newlyweds and when they would be home. They talked about the murder of Harvey Glavin. It turned out that Brian had felt the same way about telling the newlyweds about the murder. He felt that the news could spoil their trip and there was nothing they could do about it anyway. "I just hope they will be home in time for the funeral. When is it, do you know?"

"The wake will be Saturday. Then we plan to take the ashes on our Sunday ride. Will they be home for that?"

"No, I'm afraid they won't."

"They will be home for the scattering of the ashes, because we will wait for them. The wake and the Sunday ride are things that have to be done at a certain time. I'm sure Harvey would understand."

"I'm not sure," said Bridget. "I distinctly remember Harvey saying one time that the only excuse for missing a Sunday ride is death." Then she realized what she had said and apologized for what seemed to be an insensitive remark.

To change the subject, Charles asked what Brian had been doing to pass the time while the newlyweds were gone. "I've spent some of my time fixing up the apartment over the garage. I've decided to stay around here," he said looking in Bridget's direction, "and I'm going to need a place to live. I'll be working with Shane so he and Anna suggested the garage. The apartment was built before Anna and her husband bought the place, but it hasn't been used since. I don't need much, but the plumbing and electricity need to be checked and the kitchen needs work. Not that I plan to use it much."

Fiona and Bridget exchanged a look that meant, "So much for Anna's garage apartment."

"Great. Welcome to Graent," said Charles raising his wine glass. The others joined in the toast.

"I came here tonight for a reason," said Brian. "Well, I came here for a couple of reasons. For one thing I was going stir crazy all alone in that big house. For another, May keeps feeding me huge amounts of food and I swear I have put on ten pounds since Anna and Shane left. Of course, then you feed me pizza, so that didn't work out the way I thought it would. But the main reason is because I wanted to get your opinion on something. In addition to the garage, I've been working on a job for Anna. The sign over the gate to their home said Kellenwood. I know that it has to do with the last name of Anna's first husband. Shane hasn't said anything, but Anna felt that it might bother him a little, so she asked me to get rid of it while they were gone. So I did and I replaced it with something else and I wanted you to tell me what you think. I'm sure that anything that doesn't remind him of her former spouse will be fine with Shane, but I want her to like it. I have a picture of it on my mobile." He held it up and they all gasped. He had retained the slight arch of the sign with parallel curved lines which had previously held the letters of the name, and he had inserted five horses, each with its legs in a different position and giving the impression of a horse at a canter.

"That is perfect!" said Fiona.

"It's a work of art," said Charles. "Really beautiful."

"And what do you think?" he said quietly to Bridget.

"I'm almost speechless."

"Almost?"

"I am finding it hard to explain it. I can't think of anything that they would like more than that."

"I wanted to create a sign that would represent their new life together." With that Bridget excused herself and left the room.

"Did I say something wrong?" Brian asked.

Charles and Fiona looked at each other and then she said, "Bridget left her husband tonight. I guess the idea of a new life for Anna and Shane pushed a button for her."

"I'm sorry if I said the wrong thing. She's a nice person. We had fun at the wedding and I enjoyed her company. Please tell her that I didn't mean to upset her." He got up to leave. "Thank you for the dinner and the conversation."

Fiona said, "You know that sign is truly beautiful. How did you make it?"

"I dabble in metal sculptures. I use a laser tool for small shapes like these."

"You should teach a class at the Arts Center. Does Anna know you can do this?"

"I don't see how she would. I'm not even sure Shane knows. She has no idea that I planned to replace the sign and not just take it down."

"Well, they both will know about your skills soon and I will bet you cash money that Anna will try to recruit you."

"I might actually enjoy that."

Brian left to go back to Anna's house for the night and Charles went to bed leaving Fiona to clean up the few dishes and pour another glass of wine for herself and one for Bridget. She took the glasses upstairs to the guest room and the two women talked for hours before turning in.

16

Charles went to the office in the morning leaving Fiona and Bridget at the breakfast table. They finished eating scrambled eggs and toast and cleaned the kitchen before they left to do the morning chores. They decided that a short ride would be good therapy and when they were under way they discussed Bridget's next steps. It was a good idea for her to stay in Sarah's guest house. Fiona and Charles had some extra space, but even the best of friends could begin to get on each other's nerves in such close quarters. And apparently Shane's brother Brian had taken over the apartment over Anna's garage. The other thing that had to be decided was what to do with Bridget's horse.

When they finished their ride and took care of the horses, they called Sarah and told her what had happened. She took charge immediately. She said Fiona and Bridget should drive to her house that morning. She said Bridget should call the stable where her horse was being boarded to let the owners know that a Braunleaven trailer would be there shortly to pick up her Quarter Horse mare and her equipment. The horse would be taken to Sarah's stable and settled in there. She also said that she had anticipated that Bridget would leave Daniel and had had the guest house prepared for her.

"Since you will be living there alone, I had them just get the ground floor ready. There is a bedroom and bath on that floor. If you decide that you want the second floor or even the third, you can ready it after you move in. There's plenty of room downstairs, though."

"The ground floor will be enough for me. We'll be there as soon as we get cleaned up. We have just been riding and mucking stalls. Give us about two hours."

"We can have lunch at the big house and then we'll move you in."

"Thank you so much. You really are a good friend."

"You and Fiona and Anna did so much for me after Henry died. You made me feel welcome here, and I will never be able to adequately repay you for that."

Fiona and Bridget both drove their own cars and arrived at

Sarah's house at noon and were buzzed in through the front gate. They drove up the driveway past the guest house where Bridget would be living for the foreseeable future and approached Sarah's home. It was grand and stately and would have had plenty of room to accommodate Bridget without the two of them getting in each other's way. But privacy and solitude were important to Bridget and Sarah knew that. She also knew that she would be close by should Bridget need to talk.

Sarah's housekeeper, Clara, had cooked a batch of beef stew and had homemade bread hot from the oven. She knew the situation because Sarah often confided in her. "Comfort food," she said as she put the food on the table and gave Bridget a pat on the shoulder.

They enjoyed the meal together and when it was done the three of them went to the guest house, Bridget in her car and the other two in Fiona's. They carried the suitcases and boxes from Bridget's car into the house. It was a beautifully maintained home dating from the mid 1800's. The first Henry Braunlea had intended this as the main house, but his father-in-law felt it wasn't grand enough for his daughter, and had seen to the construction of the larger house in which Sarah now lived. The walls were a combination of paper and paint and the floors were made of hardwood with tile in places like the baths and the kitchen. The draperies were heavy and until they were opened completely darkened the interiors. There was a formal sitting room, a large dining room, a study with a desk that would accommodate her laptop computer, a half bath for guests, and a large bedroom with a walk-in closet and washroom with a soaking tub at one end of the room. This was a later adjustment to the floor-plan to accommodate temporary guests like Bridget, who would appreciate not having to use the upstairs rooms. The house was full of furniture that was from an earlier time, but it was comfortable and in perfect condition. The kitchen was up-to-date and roomy with a dining nook; it was also completely stocked with food in the cabinets and refrigerator.

"You didn't have to do that. I planned to go shopping later today."

"This place is yours for as long as you need it. You should take your time and decide what you'd want to do. It has been sitting empty for so long. It really is a waste. Clara made the bread and the scones, and there is a container of more of the stew she made us for lunch, but everything else came from the Braunleaven storehouse. That includes the meat and cheese, milk, vegetables, well you know." Sarah's estate was nearly self-sufficient and the goods raised there were available to everyone living on the estate. It was a great perk of working there.

"Thank you so much."

"It was my pleasure."

By the time they had all of her belongings put in their places and the suitcases stored upstairs, it was time for Fiona to go home. They decided to give some thought to how they would find out about the three mystery men, and when she left Bridget and Sarah, they were headed for the stable to await the arrival of Bridget's horse.

17

On Wednesday morning, Fiona was awakened from a deep sleep with the feeling that she was being smothered. In fact it was Charles sitting by her on the side of the bed and smothering her with kisses. "What are you doing?" she squealed.

"I'm trying to wake you," he said. "I tried to think of how I would like to be awakened in the morning and this is what I came up with."

She stretched and yawned and rolled onto one elbow supporting her head with her hand. "If you are waking me with kisses then why are you fully dressed? That's called cruel and unusual, Mr. Attorney."

"I am fully dressed because it is time for me to be on my way and I'm waking you because you have allowed yourself once again to sleep past the time you should be up and heading for the stable."

"I'm up."

"Really?"

She looked at the clock and with a groan rolled onto her back. "I'm up, I promise. You can go to work secure in the knowledge that I am not going back to sleep."

"I forgot to tell you last night that the firm is planning a celebratory dinner and drinks tomorrow night. Some of the other partners won an important case that they have been working on for over a year and they want to laud it over the rest of us. So if you don't mind, I would like us to go. If nothing else it will be really good food and you won't have to cook it. I suggested the Blue Swan restaurant that you told me about the other day and we have reserved their upstairs VIP room. Shall I tell them we will be there?"

"Of course, if you want to go, I'll go. You know that I really like the people you work with and their spouses as well. Are we dressing for dinner?"

"I believe we are. It's settled then. I told them yesterday that I thought we could make it, but I wanted to check with you to be sure. Well, I'm off. Have a good day," he said as he planted one more kiss on her cheek and left the room.

"You, too," she said as she closed her eyes and rested her head back on her pillow.

"I knew you weren't getting up," he said popping his head back inside the door. The pillow she threw narrowly missed his head as he dodged out of the way.

But she did have to get out of bed. This was the type of day that she envied her friends Sarah and Anna their stable help. It would be decadent and lovely to lie in this morning while someone else carried bales of hay and mucked horse manure. However, there was no stable hand doing those jobs for her and when she got up and under way, she was glad to be able to do it for herself. She had been raised to believe that even those people who didn't have to take care of themselves should at least have the ability to do so. She would be having dinner tomorrow with some lovely people who wouldn't know which end of the shovel to hold in their hands. Any of them left to their own devices would starve for want of knowing how to cook. So with a surge of smug satisfaction, she dressed and pulled on her wellies and went off to take care of her herd. She was glad to see that Big Tim was fitting in nicely. He seemed to enjoy having other horses around him for a change.

After her breakfast and shower, she wondered what she would do with her day and then she got a glimpse of her hair in the bathroom mirror. She had wonderful, long, thick, dark-red hair and lots of it. It was, however, a bit ratty looking so she called and made an appointment with her hair dresser for a trim and after putting the dogs in with some food and water, she drove to Graent. She arrived at the *Clipper Shop* with minutes to spare and sat with a celebrity gossip magazine while she waited for Maire to call for her. "Just a trim today," she said.

"You know that's all I'll do," said Maire in her thick Irish brogue. "If you ever decide to cut off all this hair you will just have to find someone else to do it. Got something special going on? You don't come in here usually unless you're headed somewhere fancy."

"Just a dinner with my husband's colleagues. I looked in the mirror and felt like my hair was getting a bit out of control."

"So are your nails, my darling. Would you like me to fancy them up for you?"

Fiona looked at her fingers and nails and recognized those of a stable hand. "I think that would be a great idea," she said. She'd have to be extra careful of them until dinner tomorrow evening.

After the trim and the manicure, she paid her bill and handed Maire a handsome tip. Then she thought of the dresses in her closet and decided to shop for something different from her usual attire. She was a vintage shopper and usually she wasn't overly concerned with what other people thought of the way she dressed, but she wanted Charles to be proud of her so she stopped in the shop two doors down from the salon and found a beautiful Kelley green dress that showed off her assets without being too dramatic. It was sleeveless with a slightly low-cut fitted top and a flowing full skirt and was the color of her eyes. She had a pair of emerald earrings and a large emerald dinner-ring that would match it perfectly. She then went to the shoe store and bought a pair of silver pumps that would go well with her silver evening bag. The weather predictions were for fine weather the next several nights so if she needed anything for a cover she would wear her tan and red flowered silk shawl. Feeling confident with her choices, she went home.

There were no plans for the three friends to lunch or investigate this day. Bridget was planning on going to get more of her things from the home she shared with Daniel and take them to Sarah's guest house. She also needed time to do some banking and she had an appointment with her attorney. There were many details involved in ending a marriage and she wanted to get things done as quickly as possible. She and Daniel had decided not to involve Charles, partly because they felt it would put him on the spot, and partly because they wanted to keep some things private among even the closest of friends. Sarah also had a busy day planned. In addition to her normal estate matters, she had promised hands-on attention to the Graent Arts enter while Anna was away. So Fiona decided on some jobs around the house that she had been putting off and that would not interfere with her new manicure, and when Charles returned home in the evening, she had already taken care of the barn chores, using gloves to protect her new nails, and had cooked some steaks on the grill with baked potatoes and asparagus. Some freezer rolls and wine completed the meal and they ate outside in the cool evening breeze. It was perfect.

"I found out some information today about Harvey Glavin's

brother, Andrew," said Charles, putting his feet up on the gazebo rail.

"Oh, please. What did you learn?"

"I had a meeting with a client who is buying a large piece of property. The seller had brought his attorney with him and when the meeting was over he started to talk about Harvey. He knew that I knew him and that I had been the one to find his body. He made an odd comment and I asked him to elaborate."

"What did he say?"

"He said that while he understood that I was a friend of Harvey's, he felt that there were many people who weren't exactly sorry to hear about his death. Some of them probably weren't even surprised that it had been murder. So naturally I asked him to explain. He said that when Harvey was a younger man, he was arrogant, selfish, demanding, and some would have called him a bully. He then said that there were many people who had a grudge against him, but he doubted his brother would have done it."

"Did he go into detail?"

"He did. Apparently Andrew had been a school friend of this man's brother, and the two of them have kept in touch all these years. In fact, when he found out that he could not stay in the house he was going to inherit because it was still a crime scene, he went to stay with this man's brother. The story goes like this. When Andrew was kicked out by Harvey, he had no prospects. Remember that his father had invested everything in Harvey and did nothing for Andrew. So he had no advanced education and no one around here would take him on for fear that his brother would use his newly inherited influence to make them regret it. The family attorney took pity on him and secured him a position on a ship without letting Harvey know about it. Cruise ships were all the rage back then with the upper class, and education or no, Andrew had been brought up in a cultured environment and he knew how to act and speak properly.

"He worked on ships for years traveling the world going from port to port. I gather if there's a city on Earth with a port on an ocean or a sea, then he's been there. One advantage of that kind of work was that he was nowhere near his brother. As far as he knew until recently, Harvey never knew where he ended up. He has no family because it is difficult to have a wife and children on a ship, but he has had a fulfilling life just the same. He has put aside some money since it doesn't cost anything to live on a ship, and he intends to auction the contents of the house. He also plans to divide the land and sell it in building lots. The one thing he is determined to do is tear down the house. He is adamant about that. His attorney believes that when the dust is settled, Harvey's brother will be a wealthy man, but he doesn't seem the sort to put a lot of importance on money. He told his friend that he had seen what money can do to people, and having gone without needing money for so long, he just wants to be smart with what he has."

"You said you liked him when you met him. Do you think he is not the one who killed Harvey?"

"I won't go that far. There are some killers throughout history who have been considered to be quite affable except for that whole murder thing. I just feel that he shouldn't be accused and convicted based on the fact that he wasn't treated well many years ago."

"Understood. I would like to know the gamekeeper's story, too. Have you learned anything about what he's been doing all these years?"

"I gather from Garda Simms that he fell on hard times. He had some relatives north of here with a hotel and he went there to work as a handyman. There was property with the hotel and he used his gamekeeper skills to take guests on bird hunts. It wasn't great work, but he had a place to live in the hotel staff quarters and he was fed his meals, so he got by. He didn't have the privileged background that Andrew had so his prospects after being fired weren't all that good. Few people still had estates large enough to require a gamekeeper and those who did would have wanted a reference from his former employer, and Harvey wouldn't have given him one."

"When did you learn all of this?"

"I talked to Simms yesterday, but if you will remember you were quite busy with other matters. By the way, did you do something different with your hair?"

"Why, thank you for noticing, sir. I got a trim today. Do you like it?"

"I always like it."

With that they carried their dinner plates into the kitchen and while Charles rifled through the freezer looking for ice cream, Fiona cleaned up and put the dirty dishes in the dish washer. Charles ate out of the carton until she was finished and they went upstairs together. They had had such a long conversation over dinner that the sun had gone down long ago and they were ready for sleep.

18

Thursday morning Fiona went through her morning routine and by the time she had had her breakfast and taken her shower, there was a knock on her door. She looked out the window to see who might be paying her an unexpected visit. She opened the door to Bridget and Sarah who had been to the bakery in Graent before going to Fiona's. "We brought cupcakes," said Sarah.

"Come in. I will make some coffee to go with them," said Fiona.

They gathered around the island in the kitchen waiting for the coffee to be ready while Fiona found plates and mugs and spoons. As she put the three extra-large cupcakes on the plates and they decided on who would get which flavor, Fiona poured the coffee. They put the fixings in themselves and carried plates and mugs to the sunny room on the back of the house. Fiona let out the dogs, who were salivating at the smell of their desserts.

After they all pronounced the cupcakes worth every calorie, Bridget began with an update on her situation. She had visited with accountants and bankers, as well as her attorney and things were being settled with Daniel quickly.

"I can't believe that this is all happening so fast," said Fiona. "I know of people getting a separation or a divorce who have waited months to get to this point."

"We're both ready for the marriage to be over. Daniel let my attorney know exactly what there was for assets and what we needed to square with debtors. He has apparently been expecting this to happen for at least as long as I have and he has prepared for it. He even has a buyer for the house. There won't be much money left over after the mortgage and other bills are paid, but we won't owe anything to anyone. So, it looks as if things will go smoothly and within a relatively short period of time I will be able to start the next phase of my life, whatever that is."

"What about nursing? What would you have to do to get back into it?"

"I have kept up with my licensing."

"What about skills and any changes that have taken place in

the field since you last worked? Do you get any credit for the volunteer work that you have been doing?"

"Yes, and that is the reason, other than the fact that volunteers are needed, that I did that. I never felt that I would need to go back to work after Daniel and I got married, but when I announced that I was leaving my job, my supervisor from the hospital advised me to keep up with the requirements. She told me that there were no guarantees in life and no matter how certain my future looked at that time, there might come a day when I would regret letting that license go. She's the one who signed me up to volunteer so that I would have the ability to say my skills were current. The next time I see her I am going to thank her for that."

"What chance is there that you will be able to go back there for work now?"

"To be honest, I think I would find it hard to go back to the chaos of the hospital. I would like to find a position in one of the smaller specialty clinics in the area. I wouldn't even mind a place like St. Gerald's that caters to older people. I've been to see my grandmother several times and I think the people are so charming and so grateful for the help they get there that I would enjoy it a lot. The money wouldn't be as good, but it would be good enough. Daniel and I had a beautiful home and we had beautiful things, but I look forward to living on my own and just enjoying the simple things. If I want to surround myself with luxury I'll just go to Sarah's house."

The three of them laughed at that reference to the opulence that Sarah had inherited. "What about where you will live? I know you have Sarah's house for as long as you want it, but will there be a time when you will want your own place?"

"There will, but first things first. I have to get that job before I think about anything else."

"There is no hurry about that, as you know," said Sarah.

"I know and I'm so grateful for that. It really removes a lot of the pressure I was feeling. But enough about my problems. Can we talk about Harvey's murder? Do you have anything new to report?"

Fiona told them what Charles had told her about Harvey's brother and the gamekeeper. "It seems to me that both of them have strong motives for retaliation. I can't say that they have motives for murder, because I don't think there is anything that gives someone the right to commit murder, but both of them have had their lives drastically changed for the worse because of Harvey's arrogance."

"Revenge is one of the most common motives for murder," said Bridget.

"I would like to track down the boyfriend, but I don't even know his name," said Fiona.

"He hasn't even been seen around here, has he? According to my Gran he left many years ago and hasn't been heard from since."

"I don't know. To find out if he's been here we need to find out who he is and who he knows. We need to learn if he still has friends or family left here."

Sarah asked, "You have met the brother and the gamekeeper, haven't you?"

"I have. I didn't get a good impression from either one of them, but Charles likes the brother. He seems to think that he came to grips with his life and has been happy in spite of the way he was treated by Harvey. But he admits that that doesn't mean he didn't kill him."

"So how do we ferret out the boyfriend? He was a friend of Elizabeth's family. Maybe there is someone left who knew her parents, or maybe we can find someone who went to school with her. He and Elizabeth would have been younger than Harvey, but we don't know how much younger."

"Bridget, remember the woman who worked at the school and who helped us find out the names of Winnie's parents? Would she know?" When Anna had found the body in the car on her grandfather's property, Bridget's friend had been the one to identify the murderer from old school book photos.

"I will go and call her right now."

Bridget stepped away from the table and called her friend on her mobile phone. She returned shortly and said that she had left a message for her to call. She said she would let the others know whatever she found out.

Bridget and Sarah finally pushed themselves from the table and took their dishes to the kitchen for Fiona and said it was time they left. The cupcakes and coffee had been their lunch and they were returning to Braunleaven with things to do. Sarah had a company meeting that evening, Bridget was going to continue unpacking more things she had taken from her former home, and settling into the guest house, and Fiona told them that she had a social gathering with Charles' colleagues. They made plans for their Friday lunch at the Gentry and said good-bye until then.

19

Charles had told her that he would be home at about 5:30 and that the dinner and drinks at the Blue Swan started at 7:00, so Fiona took care of the horses early and was showered and in her robe when he got home. They hoped to leave at 6:30 so he rushed up to shower and change. Charles was over six feet tall with thick steel-gray hair. He had a short professional haircut, but there was a hank of hair that tended to hang onto his forehead. It made him look younger and a bit roguish. He dressed for dinner in a dark-gray city-cut suit with a crisp white shirt and a red power tie. He wore black slip-on shoes with a matching belt. He was extremely handsome, but he didn't act like he knew it. He wore his gold wedding ring, gold Claddagh cuff-links, and a gold Rolex President watch. He didn't wear it very often, but this was a special occasion. He had bought it two years ago for Christmas and he had bought one for Fiona as well. They didn't indulge that way very often, but the look on her face had been worth the price.

He went down the stairs and caught his breath. Fiona stood in front of the fireplace in the sitting room looking strikingly beautiful. She had changed into her new green dress with the silver shoes and the emerald jewelry. She wore her own Rolex watch with a diamond band. Her thick mane of hair was loosely curled and clipped on one side with a silver comb. Her silver purse and her shawl were lying on the sofa waiting for her. She was a vision.

"Do you like my new dress? I went shopping yesterday," she said holding up the hem of the skirt with each hand and twirling 360 degrees.

"I like it so much that I want to take it off right now. You look spectacular," he said crossing the room and circling her waist with his arms.

"I know it isn't my usual style, but I wanted you to be proud of me in front of your colleagues."

"First of all, I am always proud of you no matter what you are wearing," he said standing back to take in the whole effect. "Second, they are all going to be jealous. The women will wish they looked like you, and the men will wish their wives looked like you."

He tightened his arms around her waist and pulled her closer.

"You look mighty handsome yourself, sir. I think we make a good pair."

"I've known that since the first time I laid eyes on you. May I kiss you or would it ruin that perfect make-up?"

"You may kiss me on the cheek and save more for later."

"Let's get going before I decide to keep you all to myself tonight. I can't wait to show you off."

They arrived at the restaurant as the parking lot was beginning to fill. They walked arm in arm to the front door and were greeted by Jane Lindley. After Fiona introduced her to Charles, she asked, "Are you the one responsible for this group choosing us for their celebration?" she asked.

"I did rave about it and my husband suggested it to his colleagues."

"Thank you both so much. This will give us great exposure. The next time you and your friends join us for lunch, it will be on the house."

"That's not necessary. Maybe we'll have a complimentary drink."

She showed Charles and Fiona the way to the upstairs room and they joined the party just getting started. The room was divided in half with one long table set for all the members of the party. It had a white table cloth and blue and white China, different and daintier than that used downstairs for lunch. The napkins were light blue and folded in the shape of swans. There were low center pieces with blue and white flowers and votive candles. The other half of the room was equipped with a fully stocked bar and drinks were on the law firm. Charles and Fiona said their hellos to several of the assembled company and Fiona began a conversation with the wife of one of the attorneys. She was the painting instructor at Anna's art center and she talked about how much she was enjoying working with her enthusiastic students. Just as Charles approached with a glass of wine for Fiona, she turned to notice some movement outside the window in the parking lot. "You know, dear wife," he said, "you and your dress are attracting a lot of attention." He then noticed the shocked expression on her face. "Fiona, what is it?"

She pointed to the window and Charles followed her finger. His reaction was just as strong as hers. "Did you know about that?"

he asked.

"No. This is a total surprise." What they had seen was Bridget walking into the restaurant hand in hand with Brian Anderson, Shane's handsome brother.

"That was fast."

"Yes. Do you think this started before or after she left her husband?"

"Good question."

A founding partner called for everyone's attention, made a brief speech and asked everyone to be seated so they could begin to heap praise on the group responsible for the celebration. As they approached the table, Fiona couldn't resist a brief survey of the restaurant below, and there, seated at an out of the way table, were Bridget and Brian holding hands on top of the table and sharing what appeared to be an intimate conversation. As Fiona took her seat in the chair that Charles had pulled out for her, she said to him, "I guess I know what we'll be talking about tomorrow at lunch."

20

Friday morning Fiona awoke before Charles. She looked at her beautiful new dress that had been thrown hastily onto the floor along with Charles' suit and shirt and she smiled. He had said before they left for the party that the dress was so beautiful that he wanted to take it off of her, and he had done just that as soon as they got home. She looked lazily at the alarm clock and sat bolt up in bed. "Charles! Wake up!"

"What's the matter?" he asked.

"You forgot to set your alarm clock! You're going to be late for work!"

He reached his arm over and lay it across her waist and said, "The big boss said last night at the party that we could be a bit late going in this morning."

"You should have told me. I was in a panic."

"Really. Is your heart pumping fast?" he asked pulling her closer to him.

"It is."

"Well, let me see if I can calm it down a little bit." He pulled her toward himself and kissed her full on the lips.

"That's not exactly going to calm me down."

Both were still naked from the previous evening's activities and they took full advantage of it. Sometime later, Charles dragged himself to the shower while Fiona went downstairs to fix him a hearty breakfast.

"This is a lot of food," he said looking at the eggs, sausages, fried potatoes, toast and coffee that she placed on the counter in front of him when he made it to the kitchen.

When he sat on the stool facing her, Fiona said, "You have expended a lot of energy in the last hour. I thought you might need some extra nourishment," she said pushing the lock of hair off his forehead.

He ate his fill and grabbed his car keys. As he walked behind her on the way to the garage he kissed her neck and said, "I'm going to have to take you out and get you drunk more often."

"Bye. Have a good day."

"It's started off well. See you for dinner."

Fiona left the dishes and went up to change into her barn clothes. Her cleaning lady would be arriving soon and she wanted to hang up the clothes they had thrown on the floor the night before and go to the stable before she arrived. She was a lovely woman, but she enjoyed talking more than she enjoyed cleaning. If she got Fiona involved in a conversation, the house wouldn't be cleaned and Fiona would be late for lunch. And this was one lunch she didn't want to miss.

Fiona went to the barn with the two dogs at her feet and she went through the chores with her mind on something other than her horses. How did Bridget and Brian get together? They had said they enjoyed each other's company at Anna's wedding. They had danced together several times. Had there been signs when he showed up here the night they shared a pizza? She hadn't noticed any, but Bridget had just told her she had left her husband and that had been the focus of the night. She wondered if Sarah knew what was going on. One thing she knew for sure was that she was going to find out the answers to all of those questions at lunch.

She finished her chores and went into the house and ran up the stairs. She was going to shower and dress for her lunch at the Gentry so that her cleaner knew for certain that she had somewhere to be. She put on a pair of slim black slacks and some black sandals. She found a bright blue shirt and a gray jacket and felt good about her look. She had missed Charles' shirt on the floor when she picked up earlier and as she carried it to the laundry hamper she held it to her nose and inhaled deeply the scent that lingered on it. She thought, not for the first time, about the troubles her friends had had in their marriages and she felt fortunate.

Sarah had been deserted by her first jerk of a husband, and after finding contentment with Henry, she'd lost him to cancer. Anna's seemingly ideal marriage had fallen apart when her husband fled the country to escape prosecution for defrauding clients at his accounting firm. He had left her the day after she had been taken hostage and robbed at knife point, and she thought she was going to have to raise an adopted daughter on her own until she connected with Shane. Now Bridget's marriage was falling apart, and she was going to have to go back to a career she left long ago in order to survive on her own.

How had Fiona been so lucky? She had the only man in the world she had ever loved and she was certain of his devotion to her. He proved it to her on a daily basis. She left the room thinking about how unfair life was for some, and how others had it made. She felt blessed.

She arrived at the Gentry before the others and was seated at their usual table. She ordered their glasses of Braunleaven wine and waited for the other two to show. She didn't have to wait long, and after they toasted the lunch she said, "So, what's new?" turning to look at Bridget. Was that a blush on her cheeks?

Sarah told about the meeting they had had and how her corporation had decided to donate a substantial amount of money to the Graent Arts Center so the lessons that people were receiving could continue and even increase. That was great news and she knew Anna would be delighted when she got home, but that was not what Fiona wanted to know about.

"Bridget? Is there anything new going on with you?"

"No, not really. How about you?"

"Well, Charles and I went to a lovely dinner and drinks last night."

"Oh really. Where?" asked Sarah.

As Bridget lifted her glass to her lips, Fiona said, "At the Blue Swan." Bridget did what would be referred to in the movies as a spit take. Bridget's drink flew across the table and landed on the table cloth opposite. She said, "I'm glad I ordered white wine."

"What was that about?" asked Sarah.

"I think I know, but Bridget should be the one to tell you," said Fiona.

"A person can't keep any secrets around here."

"Why do you want to keep secrets from your friends?"

"Okay. I had a date last night."

"What?" Sarah said, answering one of Fiona's questions. She clearly had not known about it.

"Look, I know it's soon, but Daniel and I have been together but apart for so long that I have had no male companionship in about three years. I don't mean I want to jump into bed with someone; I just enjoyed having a man to talk to and to make me feel like he wanted to spend time with me."

"It looked pretty intimate to me," said Fiona. "You should tell Sarah who it was you were holding hands with in the restaurant."

She looked at Fiona and then at Sarah and said, "It's Shane's brother. We met at the wedding and he was so much fun, and then we met again at Fiona's house and when he found out that I had left Daniel he called me." She paused briefly before saying, "I know what you're thinking."

"I'm not sure you do," said Sarah. "Anna and I discussed you and Brian when we saw you dancing at the wedding and agreed that he was a better fit for you than Daniel. The look on your face when you looked at him that night was happier than I'd seen on you in a long time."

"Exactly. I couldn't be more pleased for you. I think he is a really nice man and he would treat you well, if the way his brother treats Anna is any indication," added Fiona.

"You aren't mad at me?"

"I didn't say that," said Fiona. "I am furious that you felt you couldn't tell me about it after all the years we've known each other."

"Right. We don't have the history that you and Fiona have, but I am your friend and whatever you decide to do, I will support you. That doesn't mean that I won't tell you if I think you are doing something stupid, but this is not stupid. This is great."

"Right. Don't blow it."

Sarah said to Fiona, "Why not?" and they all laughed at the naughty joke that was so unlike Sarah.

"Let's talk about something else," said Bridget raising her eyebrows. "I heard back from my friend who knows everything there is to know about the people who live around here. Elizabeth Glavin was several years younger than Harvey, but just a few years older than my friend. So she remembers Elizabeth and her boyfriend. She says that he was more than a boyfriend; he was a best friend, too. They were always together to the extent that neither of them had any other real friends. His name was Kieran Hooper. One thing she remembered was that he was really intelligent. People at his school expected great things for him that fell apart when Elizabeth married Harvey. She also says that no one has seen or heard from him in years. She emailed an old picture of him and I printed some copies." She handed one to each of her friends.

"We need to tell Garda Simms about this person. Maybe he's been away all this time and came back to get even with Harvey. If so he might have gotten a hotel room or rented a car. Maybe he can be found that way," said Sarah.

"Maybe he'll be at the wake tomorrow."

"No way. He would be crazy to show up there if he had anything to do with the murder."

"He's not a suspect as far as I know. He may just fit in with the crowd and hide in plain sight to find out what progress is being made."

"At any rate," said Fiona, "I'm going to give Charles the name and the photo and he can get them to Garda Simms. This is twice this friend of yours has helped identify people relevant to a murder investigation. Garda Simms ought to hire her."

They all laughed at that as they left their seats and walked out into the hotel lobby. Sarah had left her Mini Cooper at her offices and walked out the front door while Fiona and Bridget went to retrieve their cars from the hotel parking lot. As they walked down the stairs Bridget's mobile phone rang. "Hello. Yes, I can be there in about fifteen minutes. I'm just leaving the Gentry. Bye."

"Another date with Brian?"

"No. Daniel wants me to meet him at his attorney's office. I guess there must be yet another paper for me to sign. And the date with Brian is not until 7:00," she said suddenly looking several years younger.

21

Fiona called Charles and told him about Kieran Hooper. She told him there was an old photo of him and that she wondered if Garda Simms should be told. Charles told her he would call him right away. She had shopping to do. Friday afternoon was the time she stopped at several different food markets to restock the refrigerator for the week. So it was over an hour before she left Dublin for nearby Graent. When she got home she put away the groceries and took the dogs with her for a walk to get out of the way of her cleaning lady. She picked up some stray twigs and branches that had fallen off the trees in the yard due to a strong wind during the night. As she worked she thought about Bridget and her new friend, she thought about Harvey and the boyfriend that Elizabeth left behind and the unhappiness that situation had brought to everyone concerned. She even thought that Harvey himself must have been unhappy to think that his wife preferred at least two other men. That thought didn't last long because she was really starting to dislike Harvey. Then she thought of dinner. She looked at her watch and decided to go in and put something in the oven. Surely she would have her home to herself now. She thought for just a minute about letting the woman go and doing the cleaning herself. That was just not going to happen. She didn't allow herself many luxuries, even though she could afford to, and this one she was not going to do without.

Just as she was putting a chicken casserole in the oven, Charles walked in the door. "That looks good," he said putting his arm around her waist and kissing her on the cheek.

"It will be ready in an hour," she said.

"Then I'll go change and we'll take care of the horses together." He went upstairs and came down shortly after in baggy khaki shorts and a torn tee-shirt, a stark contrast to the dark blue suit he had worn moments before. She wondered if the people who worked with him at the high pressure law firm would even recognize him in his barn clothes. They went to the stable and as they were about to finish, a familiar truck entered the courtyard pulling a trailer with the logo of the stable where Bridget and Daniel kept their horses. Daniel stepped out of the truck and walked toward them, looking a bit sheepish.

"Are we still friends?" he asked from a few feet away.

"Of course," they both responded in unison.

"Look, I know that you and Bridget go way back," he said to Fiona, "and I know that you will be there for her through all of this, you and Anna and Sarah. It gives me comfort to know that, since I still do really love her. I won't be staying here. I am moving north for a new start in a new place. I've come to ask a favor of you."

"What is it?" asked Charles.

"I heard you were in the practice of taking in stray horses and I have one more for you." Daniel's horse was a beautiful light sorrel thoroughbred about 16 hands high with an even disposition. Of all the horses in their riding club, his was the best over fences. He would have been extremely valuable except that his blood lines couldn't be proven. He had been bought at a dispersal sale and Daniel paid a low price because of the mix-up with the papers.

"I don't understand."

"Bridget took her horse to Sarah's and that's fine for her, but Sarah has so many horses and they're part of a business. I thought that if I brought him to you he would get personal attention. I won't be able to take him with me and I don't have time to try to arrange a sale. I'd be eternally grateful if you would take him, at least temporarily. If you want to find a good home for him later, that's fine."

Fiona and Charles looked at each other and he said, "Here we go again. You get him out of the trailer, Daniel, and we'll get his stall ready." Daniel had brought everything with him, the horse, the saddle and bridle, etc. and they put all of those things in the tack room.

When the horse was settled in for the night in one of the end stalls, Daniel said, "There's one more thing I'd like to talk to you about."

Fiona looked at her watch and said, "I have a casserole in the oven that needs to come out now. There's plenty of it if you'd like to join us for dinner and we can talk then."

They all rode in Daniel's truck to the house and Fiona went right into the kitchen to turn off the oven. She put in some rolls to warm, and then she went upstairs to wash and to change out of her barn clothes. When she returned, Charles was bringing the casserole and had already set the table. She grabbed a bottle of wine and some glasses with one hand and a plate of rolls with the other. It didn't take Daniel long to get to the point. "I feel I owe the two of you an explanation for what has happened between Bridget and me."

"You don't owe us anything of the kind," said Charles.

"I feel I do. I want you to know that Bridget is not to blame in any way for the end of our marriage. You see, I'm gay," he said.

The roll that Fiona had been about to put in her mouth fell to her plate.

"That's the reason for the split. I know Bridget didn't tell you out of respect for me. She was very understanding about the whole thing. She knew it wasn't something I chose. Then when we met today she asked when I realized I was gay and I told her that I knew it when I was 13. She went ballistic. She started hitting me and crying. She couldn't understand how I could marry her knowing what I knew. She said I had stolen her life. Apparently she understood my situation when she thought I had realized I was gay after we got married. But she didn't take too kindly to learning that I knew beforehand."

"And you don't understand her feeling that way?" Fiona bristled a bit as she spoke.

"I loved her then and I love her now, but I thought that would be enough and it wasn't. I tried to bury my feelings, but I couldn't. Then a few years ago I met someone and we have been having a relationship ever since. He's a good man, and I'm leaving town with him. I guess I see her point, but I really thought if I tried hard enough I could make it work. I know it was selfish of me, but I didn't know what else to do. I wasn't brought up in a family that was tolerant of different lifestyles. I assure you that I never meant to hurt her."

"Oh, Daniel. I see how hard it is for you. I just have to say that by marrying her even though you knew you couldn't be a real husband to her, you were being so unfair. Surely you can see that. You kept her from finding someone who would truly love her and give her the life she deserves. But I know Bridget. Give her some time. She'll cool down and she'll realize that you were dealing with some pretty difficult feelings. She'll forgive you eventually and she will become your biggest supporter."

"I hope so. For now, though, I think it's best that I make a hasty retreat to the north. I'll get in touch with her in a month or so to see how she's doing." He got up from the table and said, "Thanks for taking my horse. It means a lot to me. I don't think I'll go to the wake tomorrow. Harvey never really liked me anyway. I think he figured out my secret and he wasn't very tolerant of 'people like me'. So I'll say good-bye and thank you again."

He left with most of his food still on his plate and with Charles and Fiona at a loss for words.

22

Harvey Glavin's wake was to begin at 1:00 and the riding club was to meet at the funeral home at 12:30. Charles had sent an email to each of the members, with the exception of Anna and Shane, to notify them of the arrangements, and everyone had responded that they would be there. They still thought of Harvey as the nice old man who rode with them every Sunday instead of the total bastard he had turned out to be. Those who knew his true nature had decided to keep it to themselves. After all, they didn't want to have the knowledge that they had, so why would they inflict it on their mutual friends?

They assembled in the room featuring Harvey's urn. He had purchased the container himself several years ago and had stipulated that it be used to store his ashes until they were spread and it was then to be destroyed. It was left to Charles to carry out these wishes. In addition, he told the assembled crowd, Harvey had wanted the riding club to carry his urn on the Sunday ride following his death. That had not been possible because of the investigation into his murder and the fact that his body was not released by the garda in time. They would, however, be carrying his urn on the ride the next day. His ashes were to be spread in the family cemetery on the estate on the day of the ride, but since his home was still a crime scene they would have to postpone that as well.

They discussed the meeting time for the ride the next day and then the doors opened letting people in to pay their respects. As the group broke up Fiona found Bridget and took her aside. "I thought you should know that Daniel came to see us last night and he told us everything."

"What do you mean, everything?"

"He told us he was gay."

"Can you believe him? That bastard lied to me for all those years. He just wanted to use me to trick people into thinking he was not gay. I am furious with him," she whispered angrily. "I feel so betrayed."

"I know. It was horrible of him. I can not come to grips with his doing that to you. I don't blame you one bit for being angry."

"He doesn't even understand the difference between learning about it after we married and knowing since he was 13 years old."

"I know. What he did was unforgivable. You are well rid of him. He should be shot."

"Well, it was horrible, but I don't think he should be shot. That's a bit extreme."

"Why? After the way he used you, he should pay big time."

"I agree, but let's remember he was dealing with something we can only imagine. He's a good person and he deserves some slack."

"How can you say that? I'd want him to fry."

"Come on, Fiona. I'm surprised at you. Do you really think that? He's had a terrible secret to keep all these years. Do you really think he should be punished for being who he is?"

"No," she said with a smile, "but I think you were thinking it for a while. I'm glad you got to a point where you can defend him. I told him to give you a little time and that you were the kind of person who would eventually forgive him. He is a good man. And you will forgive him. That's the kind of woman you are. You can't hate."

"You're right. I will forgive him, but I'm going to wait a while before I tell him that."

"And besides, aren't you better off now than you were a couple of weeks ago?"

"I am," she said as she saw Brian walk through the door.

"By the way, Daniel brought us his horse. Do you want him? If you do we can take him to Sarah's."

"No. He intimidates me. He's so tall and strong. I prefer my little mare. I'm sure that's why he took him to you. Don't you want him?"

"We are filling our little barn fast. We really don't need him. Daniel said that if we found a good home for him we could give him away. Or if someone offers us money for him, we'll pass it along to you. He is more yours than ours after all, and you could use the cash."

"Let's just see what happens. You might grow to like him."

"Maybe Anna and Shane should take him in case a relative

of theirs needs a horse to ride," she said with a wink.

"Very clever of you. Well, Shane got Carl's horse. Why shouldn't Brian get Daniel's?"

"I agree. We'll keep him until that decision is made. On a different subject, I wanted to talk to you about what might happen here today. I thought it possible that Harvey's brother and the gamekeeper might show up at the wake since they are both in town. I thought we could strike up conversations with them to see what we can find out about where they've been recently. But it is also possible that the boyfriend might be here as well."

"I'll get Brian to help. He can talk to anyone."

"You know that about him already?" she asked with a smile.

"Ladies. It's nice to see you both," said Brian as he took his place at Bridget's side. They explained the plan and he seemed pleased to be a part of it. "Point these guys out to me when they come in and I'll see what I can do."

"Just make sure it's a casual conversation. Start with the normal kinds of questions people would ask at a wake. 'How are you related to the deceased?' or 'Did you travel far to come here today?' That sort of thing. We would do it ourselves, but if Garda Simms comes in and sees us he would know what we were up to and he would stop us."

"Do you really think he'll be here today?"

"He might. He could be thinking the same things we are. He might come to see who shows up here today."

"Okay. I'm on it. I am the soul of discretion."

Fiona scanned the room and found that Harvey's brother was already there. She pointed him out to Brian and Bridget. Fiona wandered off to see if she could spy the gamekeeper in the crowd.

Brian walked alongside her for a moment, seeming to want an opportunity to speak to her alone and said, "I understand you and Charles saw us at the restaurant the other night. I hope you aren't upset with me. I called Bridget because you told me that she had left her husband. I wouldn't have done that otherwise. The thing is, I really like her. We hit it off at the wedding and when we went out to dinner we seemed to feel a connection. I know you are her best friend, and it is important to me that you approve of us."

"Are you asking for my consent?"

"I guess I am."

"Then you have it. Just don't hurt her or I'll make you bleed," she whispered.

"Yes, Ma'am. I have no intention of hurting her. I've been looking for her all my life."

"That's all I need to hear. She's a wonderful person and she deserves to be happy and I believe that you can do that for her, but she has been through a lot. Now, on the subject of the brother, we know why he left town and what he did for a living. What we need to do is find out why he came here at this time. Did he come because he heard about Harvey? He was here pretty soon after Harvey died. Maybe he was here to see Harvey after all those years and he got here just a little too late. We specifically need to know where he was on the Friday Harvey died."

"I understand."

"Have you seen the gamekeeper? Have you two decided on a plan?" asked Bridget as she returned to the pair.

"Yes," whispered Brian. "We are on a mission. Fiona and I have decided that you and I are a team," he said sharing a glance with Fiona. They left to make their way to Andrew Glavin.

Fiona returned to Charles' side and told him that Bridget and Brian were going to see what they could learn from Andrew Glavin. "We need to see if the gamekeeper is going to show and if he does we need to find out why he's here and when he got here. That might give an insight into the note and what the puzzle in it really means."

Charles took her by the hand and led her to a far corner of the room and whispered, "We don't need to do any such thing. You are playing with fire. Do you not remember the trouble Sarah got in when she stuck her nose into a murder investigation? And what about Anna?"

"Sarah went to the killer's home with only an old man for protection. What did she expect? This is a public place. And Anna was destined for trouble when that maniac parked his car in her yard. She didn't go looking for anything."

Sarah had solved a thirty year old murder and had made the mistake of going a bit too far in tracking the killer. He had held her and her friend Braden Ahern with the intention of killing them. They were rescued just in time by the Dundalk Gards. Anna's investigation into the killer of the man whose body had been found in her grandfather's yard had put her in a similar situation.

"They both tried to do Garda Simms' job. We will give him the picture you found of Elizabeth's childhood boyfriend and then we will sit back and let Simms go to work. I'm serious about this. If anything ever happened to you I don't know how I would survive it. Promise me you won't do anything stupid."

"Alright, I promise." She thought to herself that stupid was a subjective term. They might disagree on what actions qualified as stupid.

She went into the other room of the funeral home and talked to Sarah. She told her what Brian and Bridget were doing and what Charles had said to her. "I can see that Bridget is already talking to Andrew. I can also see that the gamekeeper is now in the room. He might know what the note meant. Can you get Brian to talk to him? If I try to do it Charles will see me and that will be that."

It was clear that Fiona was going to have to settle for talking to Garda Simms who did arrive at the wake shortly before it ended. He was thankful for the photo, but he echoed Charles' thoughts about her involvement in the investigation. He said he was talking to people at the hotels in town and in Dublin, as well as rental car companies to find Elizabeth Glavin's former boyfriend. He added that public transportation areas including the airports were being contacted as well.

When the wake ended, Fiona suggested that she and Charles, Brian and Bridget, and Sarah go to the pub down the street and have an early dinner together. Charles brought up what the three women had been wanting to ask throughout the meal. "I saw you talking to Harvey's brother," he said to Brian. "How did you happen to speak to him?"

"I was just waiting around. I don't know that many people here but I felt that Anna and Shane would have wanted me to be here and I was trying to occupy myself until Bridget was ready to leave."

"You also had a similar conversation with the gamekeeper. How did that happen?"

"Same thing."

"After you have hung around with these women for a period of time you will learn to come up with better stories than that." Brian and the three women looked down at their plates. They knew they had been caught. "So what did you learn?"

Brian began with, "I wanted to talk to the two of them and find out where they were when Harvey was killed and what reason they might give for having been in the area after so many years and just at the time Harvey was killed. They both told me the same thing. They each claim to have gotten a letter from Harvey asking them to come to visit him. The letters seem to have been identical. In both letters Harvey is supposed to have said that he had done them each a serious wrong many years ago, that his health was failing, and he wanted to make amends. He wanted to somehow set things right before he died."

"I guess that means that they didn't kill Harvey," said Fiona.

"Not necessarily," said Sarah. "How can we be sure that Harvey was the one who sent the letters? Did they save them?"

"I'm afraid they didn't, in fact the brother said he wished he had saved his because now that Harvey is dead it might have been important. So I asked the gamekeeper if he had kept his and he said no. He threw it away immediately because he had no intention of coming here to let Harvey ease his conscience. Then he thought that maybe he was going to give him some money and he could really use it so he came after all. I gather that's why he's hanging around until the will is read. But both men did tell me the same thing about the letters without having heard the other's story. That should be significant."

"So," said Bridget, "maybe Harvey wrote the letters and maybe he didn't. If not it could have been the brother or the gamekeeper bringing the other one here to be considered another suspect and deflect suspicion from himself."

"Or," said Charles, "maybe someone else altogether wrote both notes for the same reason. Someone like Kieran Hooper. I'll call Garda Simms in the morning and let him know that someone at the wake had had casual conversations with both men and just happened to mention what they had said. Understood everyone?"

"Yes, Charles," they all said at once.

When they got up to leave they said they would see each other tomorrow on the ride.

"I hope you all have a good time," said Brian.

"You aren't going?"

"I don't have a horse."

"What about one of Anna and Shane's?"

"If I do that then one of them will be left alone all day and they don't separate well. I actually tried to go for a ride on Anna's horse one day out of boredom and the other one practically took down the walls to his stall. I don't dare try that again."

"That's a danger with horses that are together all of the time. We find ourselves with a barn full of horses at the moment. If you want to go we can bring along either Harvey's horse or Daniel's. We have a three horse trailer and we can pick you up on the way."

"Do I ride the dead man's horse or the former husband's horse?"

"Let's not put too much emphasis on the symbolism. We'll bring Daniel's horse along since he's an easier horse to ride for the first time. Join us." In an aside meant only for Brian, Charles said, "If things go as I think they will, you will be joining us for our rides in the future, so you might as well start now."

So it was settled. Brian would join them, Charles and Fiona would take his horse along and pick him up on the way, and Bridget was clearly delighted.

23

Sunday morning broke with a chill in the air and the wind was blowing hard through the trees. Some horses become nervous when ridden in the wind so Charles and Fiona were a bit concerned about it, but the tendency around Graent was that when the wind blew early it usually let up considerably before midmorning. They fed all the horses and let the ones that were not going on the ride out to pasture together. They took the other three out one at a time and Fiona brushed and readied them for transport, while Charles loaded saddles and bridles into the trailer tack room. He also cleaned the stalls and put in the night's feed. They always found that it was easier to do that before they went for the Sunday ride than to do it when they returned home, often tired, and sometimes after dark.

Once that was done, they loaded them into the trailer and left for the ride picking Brian up at Anna and Shane's house along the way. They drove into the driveway under the sign that Brian had made and agreed that Anna was going to love it. It truly was a work of art. Brian was waiting for them in the driveway dressed in riding clothes and boots. He got into the Range Rover and they left for the Carson's house.

Tom and Betty Carson were a lovely couple who lived a bit far afield from the rest of the group. But with horses in trailers, the distance didn't really matter. Their home was a lovely two story brick house big enough for them to have raised four children in it, but not big enough to be considered ostentatious. Their barn was too small for stabling the visitors' horses, so the riders all tied their horses to their trailers, hung hay bags to keep them occupied, and went to the side yard for a breakfast of finger foods. They enjoyed the meal and the company and when they had toasted their hosts, they started off with Charles near the front of the company carrying Harvey's ashes. He had announced that he would begin the ride with the urn, and that he would pass it along during the ride so that anyone who wished to could take a turn. He had enlisted Brian to ride with him so the three women could ride together as they always did. Fiona strongly suspected that Charles had told him that traditionally the four friends rode together and talked throughout the ride so he should leave them alone. Brian complied and rode ahead with Charles.

"He looks good on a horse, doesn't he?" asked Bridget.

"He does indeed," said Fiona echoed by Sarah.

The main topic of conversation was Harvey's murder and the information they had already. "I was thinking that we should talk to the people still working for Harvey at the time of his death. There may have been things happening around there that they noticed but didn't think unusual at the time," said Fiona.

"I do have something to add to the discussion," said Bridget. "Brian asked Robert Callahan about the man who worked for Harvey taking care of his yard and he gave me a name and an address. The man is named Kenneth Higgins. I say we should pay him a visit tomorrow. He might be able to tell us if there had been any unusual visitors around the house lately. He can also tell us about how we can find the housekeeper. We need to talk to her."

"That's a good idea," said Sarah.

"Let me finish with my morning chores, which now involve taking care of SIX horses, and then I'll go meet the two of you," said Fiona.

"Great, and when you get there we can have lunch at the house before we go."

"Okay, but if Charles asks you, we are just having lunch and nothing more. I don't like keeping things from him, but he would worry. Now here comes Charles so ixnay on the anplay."

"Who wants to take a turn with the urn?" he said as he pulled up beside them.

"How about if I tarry and not carry?" asked Bridget.

"What if it crashes with the ashes?" asked Sarah.

"I'm afraid if I bump it, I'll dump it," said Fiona.

"I'll find somebody else," he said as he rode off.

The ride went well. The wind died down drastically, the people who wanted to all got a chance to carry Harvey's urn in honor of his founding membership in their very elite club, and everyone had returned safely. Charles and Fiona dropped Brian off at Anna and Shane's and before he got out of the car he thanked them for the day. He seemed to have genuinely enjoyed himself.

Charles said, "I'm glad you liked it. We all enjoy it so much that we don't allow anything to interfere with it. Of course, a wedding like your brother's sometimes comes along and we have to excuse the bride and groom."

"I hope to join you again. Look, I know that Bridget and her husband just split and maybe you and her other friends think we're moving too fast, but sometimes when you meet the person you're intended to be with, you just know it, and it doesn't matter what else is going on around you."

Charles and Fiona shared a knowing look and Fiona said, "Trust me Brian. We know exactly what you mean."

"I'll bet you do," he said closing the door. He stood and watched them drive away and said to himself, "I want what they have."

When Charles and Fiona got home they took care of the horses and put away the trailer and Range Rover. They got to the house and let out the dogs. Dinner was a sandwich all ready and waiting in the refrigerator and a bag of crisps. The dogs were brought back in and Charles placed Harvey's urn on the table in the sitting room.

"Let's call it a day, my love," he said.

"A long day, my love," she said.

24

The next morning Charles left for the office and Fiona went to the stable. She had five horses out together and once again she had a lone horse in the end stall with the outdoor run. The horses touched noses over the fence without incident and then went on to the business of eating. Fiona left them with confidence that they would be fine. All of these horses were veterans of many Sunday rides alongside other horses. She did a few house chores, showered and changed into jeans and espadrilles with a sloppy gray sweater. She felt casual and comfortable as she left to meet her friends.

She entered through the Braunleaven front gates and drove up to the front door of Sarah's immense home. Bridget had already walked up from the guest house so the three of them sat down to a lunch prepared for them by Sarah's cook Clara. She knew that Bridget and Fiona were fond of thick soups and the grilled cheese sandwiches for which she was famous. Therefore often when they joined Sarah for lunch that is what she prepared and that was fine with them.

To call them grilled cheese sandwiches is to conjure up visions of a bland slab of cheese food product between two slices of flattened white bread. That was definitely not the case with Clara's version of the traditional comfort food. Hers were made with homemade Irish soda bread cut into thick slices. Between them were a slice of tomato and three different types of cheese, all made at the Braunleaven Creamery. She also added some spices, but she would not tell anyone what they were. She buttered them liberally on both sides and pan fried them to a golden crisp. She served them with a potato soup with chives and bacon and cheese sprinkled on top. The three women commented on the tasty meal, and after a short time, Clara returned to the table and noticed that the plates and the bowls were empty. She asked if they had enjoyed their lunch. They each pronounced the lunch almost perfect.

"Almost perfect? What would it take to make it perfectly perfect?" asked Clara.

In unison the three women said, "Apple pie!"

It was a game they played often when they shared a meal at

The Sunday Rider

Sarah's. And because Clara had played the game before, she returned almost immediately with a tray of apple pie and coffee cups. The smell alone was almost enough to satisfy their appetites.

"Now it's perfect," said Fiona.

"Thank you Clara," said Sarah. "You've outdone yourself again."

The other two heaped praise on her as well, and when she was leaving the room, she placed a small box on the table next to Fiona. "A piece of pie for your husband, Mrs. Walker."

"Thank you. He will be happy that you thought of him."

Clara was a gem. She had worked for Sarah's husband Henry for years before Sarah came onto the scene. When Henry married her, the entire staff was ready to dislike her as a gold digger. When they got to know her and saw how much she cared for their boss and how hard she had worked to make his final days comfortable and happy, they became as fiercely loyal to her as they had been to Henry. Clara enjoyed the young people that Sarah brought to the house and she made a point of pleasing them as much as possible. They always made her aware of how much they appreciated it.

The three of them sat at the table for some time nursing their cups of coffee and feeling that resting there in total contentment and comfort might be better than going to the home of a stranger. But they were on a mission. So at last they all got up from the table and took their dishes to the kitchen and they went out the front door. They got into Sarah's silver Bentley Mulsanne. It was the car she drove whenever she wanted to impress or intimidate someone and today she wanted to do both. They left Braunleaven through the stable gate turning right toward the address they had been given by Robert Callahan. They drove for about fifteen minutes before they reached the home of Kenneth Higgins. His home was made of wood painted white with a deeply sloping roof and black trim. It was extremely small but also cozy looking and well-maintained, perfect for a man living alone. The yardman's skills were not limited to the home of his employer. The walkway leading to his front door was lined with wild flowers in an explosion of colors and smells. The three women walked from the car to the small white gate, opened it and walked down the lane to the front door. Sarah's knock was answered by a short man stooped by age, but with a pleasant smile and a thick Irish brogue. "Can I 'elp ye?" he asked.

It was Sarah who spoke. "My name is Sarah Braunlea." The Braunlea name, which was so well respected in the area, got his attention.

"Please come in, Ms. Braunlea. T'is an honor to 'ave you in me 'ome." He showed them to a small but comfortable sitting room with oversized furniture and a large Egyptian area rug. He offered them a seat and asked if they would like tea or coffee. They declined.

"These are my friends Fiona Walker and Bridget Evans. We are here because we understand that you were in the employ of our dear friend Harvey Glavin at the time of his death."

"Yes, that is true. T'was a terrible thing, that."

"We are here because we are concerned about his murder. In fact, it was Fiona's husband who found him. We wondered if you had seen anything in the days leading up to his death that might shed some light on what happened to him."

"Well, I did talk to the garda 'bout everythin' I knew."

"Yes, of course, and Garda Simms is certainly doing his best to get to the truth in this case, but we knew Harvey better than he did and we thought we might be able to recognize if something was out of place or uncharacteristic of Harvey. That would be something it would take a friend to know."

"Well, I cannot think of anythin' like that. Mr. Glavin did not make conversation with me very often. I went there and did me job and 'e paid me on time and that is pretty much the long and the short of it. Except for that one thing that 'appened on the Sunday before 'e died I cannot think of anythin' unusual."

"What was the one thing that happened?"

"Mr. Glavin was usually gone all day on Sunday and so since one day is no different from another for me, I often did me work on Sunday. Sometimes if 'e was at 'ome while I was workin' 'e would get angry about the sound of the mower or the trimmer. I 'ad some work to do with a chainsaw, so I thought I would do it on a Sunday so 'e would no' complain about it. I went there in the middle of the afternoon and got to work and I see a fellow comin' out of the 'ouse. I 'ollered to 'im and 'e just waved to me as if we were the best of friends. He walked slow as you please down the path going to the back entry. I tried to follow 'im, but 'e was too far ahead of me to start with and then I saw 'im get into a car 'e 'ad parked on that little bit of gravel near to the end of the drive. I went back to the 'ouse and found that the kitchen door was unlocked, but Mr. Glavin often left it open durin' the day. I said to meself that I should remember to tell Mr. Glavin, but I guess I never thought of it again until you mentioned it."

"Had you ever seen the man prior to that day?"

"No, but by the way 'e be'aved it looked as if 'e 'ad been there before. I guess I should have told the garda about it, but like I said, I did no' think of it again until you mentioned seein' something unusual."

"Perhaps you should call and tell Garda Simms about it. It might be helpful to him. I understand that Harvey had someone work inside the house as well."

"Yes, Susan Phipps worked for 'im durin' the week. She never worked on weekends."

"Can you tell me where she lives? I'd really like to talk to her as well."

Mr. Higgins took a small pad of paper and a stubby pencil from his shirt pocket and drew a little map to show Sarah where she could find the home of Susan Phipps and handed it to her. She thanked him and asked what prospects he had for future employment.

"I am 'opin' that 'oever takes over for Mr. Glavin will be needin' someone to work in the yard that is familiar with the grounds, as I am," he said. Sarah wasn't going to be the one to tell him that Harvey's brother intended to tear down the house and divide the land into building lots.

"Good luck to you then," she said. "And if you think of anything that we might be able to use to piece together this puzzle you feel free to contact me. I'll give you one of my cards with my phone numbers on it. Please, I would appreciate hearing from you if you could add anything to what you've told us already."

"I have a question," said Bridget. "Were you working on the Sunday Harvey was found?"

"Ah, yes. I went over and did a few odds and ends. I did not go inside the 'ouse, though."

"Did you see anything of that man on that day?"

"No. No I did not. Sorry."

He began to lead them to the door. "One more question," said Fiona. "Did you take care of Harvey's horse that day?"

"I did. I noticed that 'e was makin' a lot of noise, so I went to look in on 'im and 'e 'ad eaten all of 'is food. So I fed 'im."

"It didn't seem odd to you that Harvey hadn't done that?"

"I often took care of 'im in the mornin' when I went to work. Mr. Glavin'd been acting a bit off lately, so I just figured 'e 'ad mixed up 'is days. So I fed the horse and did not think any more about it."

"Thank you for your time," they each said in turn and left Kenneth Higgins standing on his walkway as they drove away in Sarah's car.

Between the lunch and the trip to see Mr. Higgins, the three had taken up the most of the afternoon so they returned to Sarah's. Sarah dropped Bridget at the guest house and then took Fiona to her car. She went home to her afternoon routine of fixing dinner and taking care of her growing herd of horses. But the next day they would go to see Susan Phipps and see if she had anything to say about the secret life of Harvey Glavin.

25

The next morning Fiona finished in the stable with plenty of time to spare. The plans were for Sarah and Bridget to pick her up at noon. They would have lunch somewhere before going to see Susan Phipps. So she had plenty of time to shower and change into dark blue slacks and a dark blue and white printed oversized man-style shirt. She left the tails hanging out and rolled up the sleeves and caught them with a button-tab. A pair of dark blue flat sandals and a hobo bag completed her outfit. They had not decided yesterday where they would go, but in this outfit she felt that she would be dressed appropriately for any restaurant in the area at lunch time.

It was an understated outfit, but it was chic and just right to interview someone who had worked in a big house for as long as Ms. Phipps had. She didn't want to stereotype, but if the woman had worked for years for someone as domineering and pretentious as Harvey Glavin, then it was just possible that she would be unable to resist telling someone of his social station exactly what they wanted to hear. She felt terrible about it, but she had seen before the effect that the mention of Sarah's name had on people in positions similar to that of Susan Phipps and she was, in this case, willing to use whatever advantage she and the other two women might have.

Sarah and Bridget were on time as usual and Fiona met them outside. She got in the back seat of Sarah's Bentley. They talked for a minute before they left Fiona's drive about where they would go. Sarah had a particular reason for wanting to return to the Blue Swan, and since Fiona and Bridget had both enjoyed their meals there, they agreed. They all dearly loved the Gentry Hotel, and they would certainly not allow the new restaurant to replace it completely, but it was nice to have a place to eat in Graent that had good food in a pleasant and quiet atmosphere. Pubs were great and an integral part of the culture of the area, but once in a while a nearby place like the Blue Swan was just what they wanted.

They got there at about 12:30, and the restaurant was busy for lunch. They were greeted at the door by Jane Lindley, as they had been during their earlier visits, and she gave them each a warm welcome. She spoke to Fiona and said, "It's so good to see you again Mrs. Walker. We have had so many bookings as a result of the dinner your husband's firm had here that we have had to hire more wait staff. I can't thank you enough."

"Don't thank me." Motioning toward her friends, she said, "We are just delighted to have such a wonderful new restaurant in the area. I'm glad if I had any influence on your business. These are my friends Bridget Evans and Sarah Braunlea." There was the usual reaction to Sarah's name.

Sarah spoke up then and told her how much she had enjoyed her one visit for lunch. "As you may know, I own a vineyard."

"I do know. I worked for a time at the Gentry restaurant and we served your wines there. They were top sellers."

"Then you may know that I have an exclusive area contract with the Gentry, so I can't offer you the chance to sell our wines here, but I can make a gift of a few bottles. There is a case in the trunk of my car if you have someone who can carry it in. You can give them as gifts, but you can't sell them. Don't worry about someone finding out about it, because I have already cleared it with the Gentry. Management speaks very highly of you there and they are happy for your success. I left the trunk open so you can send someone out to get them. It's the silver colored car in the parking lot."

"That is so generous of you. I can't thank you enough. Lunch is on the house today."

"That isn't necessary," they all said in unison.

"I absolutely insist. You've helped my business immensely and your gift of wine is so generous. Please let me do this small thing for you."

"Thank you very much. We accept," said Fiona.

She showed them to the same table they had shared the first time they were there and called over the waitress with instructions to give her very good friends whatever they needed.

"I feel guilty taking a free meal from someone starting out in this business. So few new restaurants actually survive," said Bridget.

"I agree," said Fiona, "but in this case I think it would have been rude to refuse her gift." Sarah agreed.

The waitress brought them tall glasses of ice water and a basket of hot rolls along with the day's menu. They all decided on a pasta dish that was offered as a special that day, understanding that ordering a meat dish would have cut deeper into their hostess' profits. They ordered tea and lemon pie for dessert and left a tip for the waitress that would have covered the cost of the meal. They made certain to make eye contact with the owner as they left and to thank her and tell her that once again the meal was wonderful. They got into Sarah's car and left the parking lot and turned right to follow the map that Kenneth Higgins had given them the day before.

"As a map maker, he's a very good gardener," said Bridget as she struggled to decipher the scribbles on the small piece of paper he had used for the directions to the housekeeper's place. "It's too bad he couldn't remember the name of her street. We could have used the GPS and I'm sure we'd be there by now." There were misses on their part as road lines and street names didn't quite match up, but somehow, perhaps by sheer luck, they arrived at the home of Susan Phipps.

26

Susan Phipps lived in a row house on a neglected side street in the town of Graent. Its architecture was indistinguishable from the other homes lining both sides of the street except for the house number next to the front door. They looked for number 12 and found it between two other homes from which the numbers were missing. This was an area of town that time seemed to have forgotten. If the road had not been paved and there had not been occasional automobiles parked along the curb, then it would have been possible to imagine this as a Victorian era setting. The bricks in some of the buildings were starting to crumble and the concrete steps leading up to several of the homes looked hazardous. The wrought-iron railings on many of them had been replaced with wood or were missing completely.

But number 12 was in perfect condition. Sarah again took the lead and lifted the wrought iron knocker. On the third knock the door was opened by a woman in her sixties wearing a house smock covered by a greasy apron. She looked beyond the three women on the stoop and caught sight of the fancy car parked out front. She couldn't have told what kind it was, but she knew it was expensive. She straightened as if she knew she was talking to someone with money and power. And when Sarah introduced herself, using her last name, the poor woman actually bowed and invited them in. She offered them tea, and when they accepted, she invited them to sit in her parlor while she fixed it in her small but tidy kitchen. They took places on solid but comfortable matching couches facing one another on either side of a distressed wooden tea table. The furniture was old, but it was of good quality and spotlessly clean. Susan Phipps returned with a tray of China cups and a tea pot that was identical to those they had all used at Harvey's home. She poured and passed around the cups and asked to what honor she owed this visit.

"These are my friends Fiona Walker and Bridget Evans. We are here because we were very close to your former employer, Harvey Glavin," she said dramatically so as to emphasize their loss. The three women saw the panic in Susan Phipps' eyes as she looked at the china service she had used to serve the tea. She had brought out her best for the elegant ladies who had come to visit, not realizing that they would recognize it as Harvey's. "We were wondering what you could tell us about him. We know you worked for him for a long time, and judging from the china that he gave you," she said with a smile as she lifted her cup, "you must have been a favorite of his." This accomplished two things. It told Ms. Phipps that she knew that the China was Harvey's and that it was not a gift, and that if she didn't give her the information she wanted, Sarah could report the theft; it also told her, if the woman wanted to take it that way, that if she gave them the information they wanted that Sarah would consider the china a gift from her long-time employer and that she could avoid trouble with the law.

"I'll be happy to tell you anythin' you want to know," she said, casting her eyes downward toward the Oriental rug that had surely once graced a room in Harvey's home.

"Good. We are interested in the sort of man he was during the years you worked for him. Was he a good employer? Did he have any particular friends or particular enemies? Just try to remember anything that might give us an idea of how people might have thought of him as a person."

Ms. Phipps thought for a few moments with a puzzled look on her face which suddenly turned resolute. "He was a bastard," she said. "I'm sorry to use such coarse language in front of you ladies, but he really was a bastard. He was so mean to poor Kenneth Higgins, the man who worked so hard for him. He treated him like he was a dog. Kenneth tried to quit several times, but Mr. Harvey told him that if he did he'd never get another job 'round here. He told me the same thing more than once. We were afraid to leave, me and Higgins, because, as he often told us, he had influence 'round here and if he told people not to hire us, they wouldn't. We'd've ended up on the dole. We had to work long hours for very short pay."

"Pardon me," said Fiona, "but both you and Mr. Higgins have lovely homes. I don't want to pry, but how could you afford them if he paid you so little?"

She was silent for a moment before she spoke. "I'm gonna tell you everythin' you want to know," she said meekly. "In return you're gonna learn a few things 'bout me and Mr. Higgins that you won't approve of."

"Mr. Glavin is dead and we are not members of law enforcement. Whatever you tell us will be our little secret. Okay?"

"Mr. Harvey had a house full of treasures and he didn't even know about 'em. There was a regular store of old kitchen utensils and sets of dishes that no one from upstairs had seen in years. Whatever was bought by the original Glavins was still down there. Mr. Harvey would never lower hisself to go down to the old kitchens and so me and Higgins decided to do the same thing that he had been doin' for hisself. He would sell things from one of the upstairs rooms to pay for repairs to the house, or he would pay his debtors off with a picture, that sort of thing. Well, we took the things from the kitchen and sold 'em to collectors on our days off. I have an old car and when Mr. Harvey was gone of a Sunday, we would go and load the boot of my car with things to sell and we would take 'em to dealers all over the countryside. We pretended to be married and we would say we were fallen on hard times and selling off the things we loved so dear to be able to stay in our home. We fairly cried to let 'em go and folks felt sorry for us. The things for the kitchen weren't given the Glavin mark so people had no way of knowin' where they come from. So me and Kenneth made up for our low wages by stealin' from him. We did pretty good, too," she said with a chuckle. "Then when the kitchen things were all gone we went to the stables and found old fashioned farmin' tools. People pay big money for those things nowadays. We found real treasures in the rubble from that old barn that fell down years ago. Mr. Harvey hadn't touched that place since it collapsed and he had no idea what was in it. What harm did it do to dig out some of those old things? After a while we got bolder and went into the house proper to find things that Mr. Harvey wouldn't think were good enough for him, but we knew others would buy 'em. We've become sort of experts at pricin' antiques because we've been to so many shops."

"I think I recognize some of Harvey's things here in this room," said Fiona. "Is that possible?"

"Yes. I don't mind tellin' you that sometimes when I look at the little things I brought here, such as them china cups you're drinkin' from, I feel happy that I was able to put somethin' over on him. You ladies might be thinkin' what we done was terrible, but in my opinion we deserved to get somethin' in return for all that we put up with over the years. Our pay was never raised and of course our bills were. So every year we were gettin' more and more behind until we come up with this scheme. We had repairs to do on our homes and debts to pay. I will not feel embarrassed about taking a little from him and he never missed any of it." Ms. Phipps was clearly becoming agitated at the possibility that the fine privileged ladies in front of her were judging her for actions that she felt were not only justified but necessary.

"I don't think I want to hear any more about the theft of Harvey's property. I don't judge you for what you did, and I'm sure that Harvey never did miss these few things, but I'd like to move on to how he dealt with other people. Did he have friends or enemies that you can think of?"

"He had no friends that I knew 'bout, other than the people who went on those stupid Sunday rides of his. He called 'em his posse. He said the rides were all about how the people of the area wanted to honor him by ridin' with him." Her voice and her facial expression told all they needed to know about how she viewed their Sunday pastime. "It was as if he thought they were obliged to go or maybe they did it only because of the love and affection they had for him. I wonder how anyone could feel that way about him, but he was convinced. He used to say all the time that no one dared miss a ride because they would know they would be disappointin' him and because of his position people wouldn't want to bring on his disapproval."

"Well, don't I feel stupid," whispered Bridget.

"Let's move along. What about enemies? Did he have any that you know of?" asked Sarah.

"He had lots of arguments with different folks. The people who went to the house to buy his carpets and paintin's was always sayin' that he was tryin' to cheat 'em. He would tell 'em that they should be honored to have somethin' from his collection. One feller told him that he couldn't charge by how grateful people felt to have somethin' of his. He didn't like that, I can tell ya. But it wasn't until just lately that he started to act like someone was after him. He began askin' if I had seen anyone lurkin' 'round the house or the grounds about a week before he died. He said that he felt like someone was inside the house. I thought he was gettin' old and senile. I thought he was imaginin' things. He also wanted to know if I noticed that anythin' had been taken. Of course I had to say no to that. But one day I asked why he kept askin'. He told me that it was none of my business, but if I noticed anythin' missin' while I was cleanin' to let him know. I said I was always noticin' things missin' because he was always sellin' things. He got real angry at me that day and told me if I didn't stop sassin' him I would be out of a job and he would replace me. I said I didn't know of anyone else who would put up with him. I thought he'd blow up, but he said he guessed I was right about that. Anyway, from some of the things he said, I got the feelin' that he thought someone had been in the house to steal from him, or maybe even to do him harm. He sometimes would take to lockin' hisself in that study of his for hours at a time like he was hidin' from somebody."

"I wonder what made him think that someone was lurking around?" asked Fiona.

"We know from what Mr. Higgins said that a man was when Harvey was gone," said Sarah. "Maybe he was there at other times and Harvey could sense that he was prowling around. Or maybe he left signs that he had been there."

"Higgins told you about him? He saw someone and he told me 'bout it so I would be careful of meself, but he said he wasn't gonna tell about it until he had to. He figured that if Mr. Harvey knew, he would hire someone to keep a look out and then our pilferin' days would be over. We decided that we would only tell Mr. Harvey if he caught on to what we were doin'. Then he would blame the intruder and not us. So I don't think that he ever mentioned it to him."

"Is there anything else you might be able to tell us?"

"I do know that he was always very secret about his study, where they say he died. He didn't want no one in there. I had to go in to clean it, but he didn't like leavin' me alone in there. I used to look in on our Sunday visits, but I could never find anythin' worth keepin' secret. One time, though, I was goin' in to clean and he was sittin' at his desk looking into a small box, like a biscuit tin. When he heard me come in he slammed it closed. Then he yelled at me to get out and not come back in until he said I could."

"We are learning about a side of him that we never knew," said Fiona. "And the more I hear, the more I want to get inside that house and look around, especially at that desk."

"I agree, but we can't get in there. The police have it guarded so no one can get into the house," said Sarah.

Ms. Phipps said, "Why don't you use the tunnel?"

The three younger women were shocked again. "What tunnel?" they asked in unison.

"I think it was somethin' that one of his ancestors had built, back when the family was religious. Course Mr. Harvey wasn't religious. Anyways, I think they used to call them Priest Holes. One time when I went in to clean the study, the room was empty," she whispered as if she had a secret to tell. "Then I turned toward the corner of the room and Mr. Glavin come in through a doorway behind a column. There were four columns in the room, one in each corner. The one in the left corner behind the desk leads to a tunnel. He was angry that I had seen him and he said to never mention that door to anyone. Of course I said I wouldn't. Only one day while he was gone I snuck in and found the switch. It's right on the book case next to the column. It's a brass figure of a horse standing on its hind legs. You pull it and the column swings open. It's big enough for a grown man like Mr. Glavin, so the three of you would have no problem."

"That's interesting, but we would need to get into the house to use it."

"No, my dear. The other end of the tunnel comes out in the stable. If you go in the enclosed stairway next to the tack room, the one that leads to the loft, there is a panel that opens to the left of the stairs and the tunnel entrance is there. The tunnel is quite long, but it is safe and when you get to the end of it the switch to open it from inside the tunnel is easy to find. Just don't do what I did and forget to take a light with you," she laughed.

They left Susan Phipps' house and got into Sarah's car. "Someone tell me what a Priest Hole is," she said. "I'm sure I never heard of anything like that in New Jersey."

"After the British invaded Ireland, they hunted priests because the British were Protestant and they wanted everyone else to be, so many priests went into hiding. They were not allowed to conduct religious services. People who hid them often had their homes burned to the ground. So when one of them went into hiding in a big house like Harvey's, the owners would have a hiding place built into the walls, or inside the stairs, or in this case, behind a column apparently. A lot of these big houses had secret passages anyway, so they would just adapt them. Sometimes they were places for the priest to stay hidden until the house had been searched and the hunters were gone. Other places had tunnels like Harvey had so they could actually escape," said Bridget. "We have got to get into that tunnel. I can't believe it. This whole thing keeps getting better and better."

"Hang on," said Sarah. "This is nothing to fool with. I say we tell Garda Simms about this. It may be how the killer got into the house."

"No," said Fiona. "The killer broke the kitchen door. The jam was in pieces and the door ajar when Charles got there that night."

"Still, going into that house could be dangerous."

"No one can get in there. We're the only ones who know about the tunnel and the house has a security detail guarding it all the time."

"We don't know that we're the only ones who know about it. The killer may have broken the door after he killed Harvey to throw everyone off guard."

"I don't think so," said Fiona. "According to Charles, the footprints that had the tea on them went from the hall to the kitchen door as if the killer was leaving by that way, but none coming the other way."

"That doesn't mean that that is how he entered the house. If the killer is Harvey's brother, he would surely know about the tunnel. And the gamekeeper would have worked there long enough to possibly know about it. We can't even be sure that Harvey's wife didn't tell her boyfriend about the tunnel so he could get in to see her. If Ms. Phipps learned about it, then any of the others working in the house could have as well, and you can be certain that news of something like that would have gone through the entire staff. People love to gossip about things like that. I don't like this at all. It is too much like me going to see a killer with just an old man for backup, and Anna would tell you the same thing. I'm telling you it is too dangerous. Garda Simms must be told about it and we need to back off. I have made my last investigation into the murder of Harvey Glavin, and I want you both to promise that you're done as well. I know that you both think Anna and I were adventurous and brave when we were held hostage, but we felt anything but. It was scary and not something I would ever want to repeat."

First Bridget and then Fiona said what Sarah wanted to hear. Fiona said she would tell Charles to call Garda Simms and tell him everything they had learned from the gardener and the housekeeper. Then Bridget said she would ask her Gran if she knew anything about the tunnel but that otherwise she would leave the case to the professionals. Sarah put the car in gear and headed for home not noticing the glance shared by the other two while her eyes were on the road.

27

The next morning Charles woke much earlier than usual and suggested that he go to the stable with Fiona to do the morning chores. When she told him that Bridget was expected to come over this morning to help with them, he suggested something else they might do since he was already awake. When he eventually got out of bed to go to the shower she said, "Thanks. Now I'm too tired to get up."

He dressed while she lay there trying to make herself move. He told her he had a big day ahead but that he would call her if it meant he would be late for dinner. Charles allowed himself to have a late day at the office once in a blue moon and he would try to avoid it tonight if he could, but there were people in town who wanted to finish their business before returning home. If that meant staying an hour longer than his usual work day, he felt obligated to do so.

He tied his tie and put on the jacket to his gray pin-striped suit and asked how he looked. He looked to Fiona like he could be on the cover of GQ and she told him so. He said, as he leaned over to kiss her again before he left, "Right now you look like you could be on the cover of Playboy." She allowed her thick mane of hair to fall across one eye, gave him a sexy pout and told him to have a nice day.

Bridget arrived about an hour later and since they were both hungry, they got some cartons of yogurt from the refrigerator and some plastic spoons and ate on the way to the barn. They fed all the horses some oats and then put them into the pasture for the day. They cleaned the stalls and filled the hay racks with slabs of hay for evening. They swept the floor, wheeled away the muck from the stalls, and put everything they had used away in the tack room. They returned to the house and Bridget got a bag of clean clothes from her car. Fiona went to her room for a shower and Bridget used the one in the guest room that had been hers just a few days ago. When they were both dressed in jeans and runners, with dark sweatshirts, they went down to the kitchen for a late morning snack of coffee and scones. Fiona found two flashlights in the kitchen junk drawer and put them on the counter.

"Are you sure we should do this?" asked Fiona.

"Don't tell me you want to chicken out."

"I just feel guilty. We promised Sarah, I promised Charles, and I was ordered by Garda Simms not to go near the place. I feel like we're betraying a lot of people. And it might be dangerous."

"How can it be dangerous? There's no one in the house. The only reason we have to sneak is because the police and the security guards are keeping everyone out. If they would just let us in to look around we wouldn't have to do this. All we need to do is go in through the tunnel, which by the way I can't wait to explore, and take a look to see if there is some hidden compartment in the desk. If there is and if there's something in there that points to someone in particular, then we will of course go straight to Garda Simms. If there isn't we leave the way we entered and no one needs to know we were ever there."

"I know. But I can't help but feel funny about it. I have butterflies in my stomach."

"We'll have our mobiles with us and we'll take care of each other. We've had each other's backs for what, twelve years now?"

"Okay, you're right. Are you ready?"

"I am."

They got into Bridget's car and they headed for the back entrance to Harvey's property where the gardener said the intruder had parked his car on the day he was seen leaving Harvey's house. They found it and Bridget parked there under some low hanging tree branches. The car was green and blended in with the leaves hanging down around it. They followed the dirt driveway for as long as they could without being seen by any of the gards patrolling the grounds in the front of the house. The barn was quite far from the house and had not been a crime scene so it had been left alone. They entered the woods when they neared the barn and approached it from the far end.

Harvey's barn was quite large. It was long and tall and at each end there was a pair of sliding doors. Each individual door was about two stories high and half as wide. A pair together made an opening large enough to bring in heavy equipment and large trucks full of hay bales. In one of the doors on each end was a normal sized entry that was used when someone wanted to go in or out without sliding the larger doors on the track. They found the far door and lifted the latch. It was close to noon but the inside of the barn was quite dark. For an old barn it was well built with little in the way of spacing between the boards. The windows were dirty from years of neglect and let in very little light. They were forced to use the flashlights to look for the secret passageway that Ms. Phipps had described. They found one ladder and two stairways to the loft but they were all open. Bridget and Fiona had been in this barn many times and had never noticed an enclosed stairway, but the housekeeper had said it was next to the tack room. They found a door there and opened it. Just as she had said there was a panel that looked a bit out of place as if it had been used to replace or repair an earlier one. They pushed on the left side of it and the door popped open toward them.

They looked at each other as if to say, "This is the point of no return," and Bridget went first through the door and down the six steps they were told they would find. The floor of the tunnel was made of concrete. Ms. Phipps had said that Harvey had had a pad poured in there some years ago to cover the dirt that had been the floor from the time it had been dug generations ago. The walls were made of stone and the ceiling consisted of square-cut rough-hewn beams placed close together for support. "This solves a mystery for me," said Fiona.

"What mystery is that?" asked Bridget.

"I have mentioned to Charles several times that it didn't make sense that Harvey had that fence across the yard between the barn and the house. It seemed to cut off what would be a natural traffic lane causing him to put a connecting road from the front entrance all the way around the end of the barn and then out the back drive. The fence is decorative, but Harvey never seemed concerned with decoration anywhere else. Now I know why it's there. He didn't want anyone to drive a heavy vehicle over the top of this tunnel."

"I'm sure you're right. When this thing was built the heaviest thing that would have gone across it would have been a horse-drawn carriage."

They covered the distance in a short time. It was hard to judge the length of the tunnel underground in the dark, but the distance from the house to the barn was about 60 meters, so the tunnel would be just a bit more than that, having to extend to the home's interior. When they reached the end and the six steps going up into Harvey's study, they located the lever that they were told would be easy to find. Bridget pulled on it and the tunnel door opened into Harvey's study. There in front of them, in a place of prominence in the room, was Harvey's desk. They looked at each other, took a deep breath, and walked toward it.

28

There was light enough coming in through the sheer curtains in the windows of the study for them to see everything in the room. The heavier panels had been left pulled to the sides, as they had been the day Harvey was killed. Bridget and Fiona were able to put their flashlights down and use both hands in their search. They were tempted to close the draperies so that they could not be seen by any garda passing by, but they were afraid that such a change would bring someone in to check on the crime scene, and they didn't want that.

They turned their attention to the desk, the top of which was neat and tidy. Fiona wondered if that was Harvey's habit or Ms. Phipps' cleaning that kept it that way. There was a brass reading lamp with a dark green globe made of thick glass, a tooled leather tray full of Harvey's personal stationary with his family insignia for a letterhead, an empty wooden holder for a letter opener, a single black Mont Blanc pen, a pewter coaster for a tea cup, and nothing else out of the ordinary. They walked around the desk looking for the possibility of a false compartment in the front. It was massive and ornately carved out of walnut. It was almost the same on both front and back, except that the single rectangular panels on both sides of the front were replaced with drawer fronts on the back. The ends were carved as well, but it did not appear that there were compartments that could hold secrets. Bridget lay on the floor to look at the underside of the desk for a closer inspection and saw nothing there either.

They concentrated their attention on the drawers, Bridget taking the left side and Fiona the right and the center. Bridget's side had three drawers and using a ruler found in the center drawer, she measured and decided that the numbers added up the way they should and that the drawers on her side had no secret compartments. Fiona's side had only two drawers, one small one the same as the ones on the other side, and though it was made to look as if it were two separate drawers, there was a double sized one on the bottom to hold larger items. Harvey had filled it with a modern metal hanger for sliding folders, but when she tried to push the front files to the back, she ran into resistance. "I think there might be something here," she said.

She separated the hanging files where the obstacle seemed to be and pulled out a metal biscuit tin. She placed it on top of the desk. They looked at it and then at each other. "What now?" asked Bridget.

"So that's what was 'down under'. It must be the box Ms. Phipps was talking about," said Fiona.

"We have a choice. We can open it now and see if there's anything in it, or we can take it with us and get out of here."

"I vote that we open it," said a man's voice behind them.

Fiona and Bridget whirled in the direction of the voice and saw before them an older version of the man in the picture Bridget's friend had given them, and he was holding a small knife along the lines of a letter opener. "You're...," said Fiona.

"I'm what?" he said.

She had been about to tell him that she knew who he was, but thought it would be better to withhold that information. "You're not supposed to be here. And you don't look well."

"Good save. I think you know who I am. I saw you giving my picture to the garda at Harvey's wake. I surely don't look the same as I did when that photo was taken, but you can see enough of me in it to know who I am." He saw the surprise in both their eyes and said, "Yes, I was there. You see, I made a mistake when I was here last. I needed to find out if anyone was on to it, and I learned a few things at the wake listening to the little conversations here and there. I learned that the gards knew who I was and what my connection to Harvey Glavin was. I learned that the note Harvey left was a trick and that there was a message in it that might identify me as his killer. It was stupid of me to let him write it. I should have known he would do something sneaky. I learned that there were three women who thought they were private detectives and that they had disobeyed the law to get information before. I decided to hang around here out of the sight and see if you would come to investigate, and you did."

"No, we're just old friends of Harvey. We wanted to get a souvenir of him before his brother tears down this old place," said Bridget.

"Another good save. But I don't believe you. What do you

suppose Harvey had in that tin you found? It's obviously something he wanted to keep hidden for whatever the reason. Open it."

"I don't think we should."

"Open it! Now!" he said with a cough.

Fiona opened the tin and found inside a collection of folded notes. She looked at Kieran Hooper and saw raw emotion in his eyes. He walked slowly toward the desk and Fiona stepped back to give him access to the box. He picked up one of the notes and slowly opened it. He read it and then he crushed it in his hand.

"These are notes from you to Elizabeth, aren't they?" asked Fiona. "We were told that her maid acted as a go between, taking notes back and forth on her days off. Are these the notes?"

He nodded his head. "I thought she was helping us. Elizabeth thought she was her friend. But she was showing all of them to Harvey. I found out the night I came to get Elizabeth that Harvey had caught her and told her he would fire her if she didn't bring the notes to him before delivering them from then on. He must have saved these after he took them from Elizabeth…"

"That's how he knew the two of you had made your plans to run away. And that's how he was planning for us to find out who his killer was."

"You have it all figured it out, haven't you?"

"No, it just makes sense. From what we've heard about you and Elizabeth, the two of you had to feel desperate, so it makes sense that you'd try to run away together. You had to have help to arrange that with her being a virtual hostage in this house."

"He took her from me. He had no right to do that. But people with money like Harvey Glavin think they have the right to take whatever they want. He took her and treated her like a prisoner. So I came here that night as we had planned. He was supposed to be at his weekly card game. When I came in through the tunnel he was waiting for me. He was so arrogant." Kieran Hooper paused here, his face a mixture of anger and pain. "He talked to me like I was dirt. He said I would never set eyes on her again. He said he could kill me and get away with it because he had caught me breaking in to steal from him. He said he might even kill me with Napoleon's sword." Kieran Hooper looked at the wall where the weapon was hanging in a place of prominence. "He took it off the wall and waved it around and then he put it back. He said

I wasn't worthy of such a noble weapon and he didn't want the publicity that my body would invite. He was old and feeble the night I came here to kill him, but back then he was big and strong. He took fencing lessons, and boxing lessons, and he rowed crew, but it was the boxing lessons that he used that night. He hit me so hard I couldn't breathe, and he kept hitting me until I couldn't stand up anymore.

"I lay there on the floor," he said walking weakly to the spot, "with blood running out of my mouth and my nose, and he just opened the door and let in two of his henchmen and told them to take me away. They dragged me out the front door and threw me in the back of a wagon. They had it all planned, of course. The last thing I saw as I looked up out of that wagon-bed was Elizabeth. She was standing in an upstairs window with the lamp on behind her. She looked like a bright shining star looking down on me. I remember thinking, 'There you bastard. You said I would never set eyes on her again and you were wrong.' I passed out then and when I awoke I was on a boat in the Atlantic off the coast of Spain." He paced as he told the rest of the story. "They had driven me to Dundalk and bribed the captain of a ship to take me to Australia.

"When I got there I tried to sneak back on the ship and the captain said that he would be no better off than me if he didn't leave me there as he had been paid to do. I had nothing but the clothes on my back. I had no money. I was in a strange country. I didn't even have a passport. One of the hands on the ship caught up with me as I was leaving the docks and gave me all the money he had. He said he was sorry for his part in keeping me on the ship and that giving me some money was the least he could do. It wasn't much but it bought me dinner that night and a hotel room until morning." He paused again, leaning on the back of the sofa. He was red in the face and his breathing was labored, but he went on as if this were his last chance to tell his side of the story.

"I was brought up without much money, but I had never been forced to sleep in a place like that. It would have been better to sleep outdoors, but I didn't dare do that in a foreign country. When I walked out of there in the morning there was a man standing in the bed of a pick-up truck. He was yelling about needing men to work for him. He said he couldn't pay anyone right away but he would when he could. He said in the meantime, he would provide three meals a day and a clean place to sleep. I walked over and climbed into the back of that truck and soon three other men did, too.

"We drove for about two hours and then we got to a sheep station. God, I hate sheep. I always have, but he had lost his wife and his son to pneumonia the winter before and he was trying to keep from losing his ranch. The first year we worked for him his entire income from the market went to repay creditors and put money away for expenses. When we took his sheep to market the next year he rewarded each of us with a large amount of cash. I hitched a ride with him back to the same town I had been in before and thanked him for the job. I stood in a line where they were hiring ship hands." He paused again for a breath. "I couldn't buy a ticket because I didn't have a passport. Anyway, as I was standing there, someone I had known from back home came walking up the deck from one of the cargo ships that had just come in from Dundalk. We said hello and he said that everyone back home had thought I was dead the way I just disappeared. I said I was headed back home to see Elizabeth. He said that he was really sorry to have to tell me, but she was dead. He said she had killed herself. I just turned and walked away and got back into the boss's truck and went back to the sheep station."

By this time Fiona was engrossed in the story to the extent that she forgot she was in the presence of a murderer, and Bridget, the nurse, was concentrating on the deteriorating condition of Kieran Hooper, wondering what was causing the weakness and loss of breath. It could, after all, be caused by a number of ailments. The more he spoke the weaker he seemed to be.

"I know she didn't kill herself," he went on. "She was religious. She would never do what she considered a mortal sin. The night I came back here I accused Harvey of killing her and he admitted it. He said she deserved it because she was having an affair. I don't believe that of her, either.

"I'd probably still be there on that sheep ranch since there was nothing left for me here, but I started having a lot of pain. The boss took me to a doctor and he said I have cancer. He said I didn't have long to live. I thought to myself, 'What is the one thing I would like to do before I die?' You know what that was? I wanted to kill old Harvey Glavin, and I wanted him to see it coming before I did it. So I bribed a ship's captain to bring me home without a passport. Ironic, isn't it?

"I came back here and watched him for a while. I even spent time here in this great monstrosity of a house while he was at home. I spent the night several times and the place is so big that he didn't even know it."

"You're the one the gardener saw leaving the house while Harvey was at a Sunday ride."

"Yes. The big man was away taking part in a leftover vestige of the aristocratic reign of terror over the working men of this country, the ride to the hounds, only without the hounds. What a joke."

He didn't seem to notice the looks on the faces of the two women as he ridiculed an institution that to them had always been just a fun cross-country ride with friends. He was right, though. His view of the ride was accurate when it came to Harvey Glavin.

"Did you send letters to Harvey's brother and the groundskeeper telling them to come here for some kind of amends?"

"I did. I had learned from the maid who brought the notes from Elizabeth all those years ago that Glavin had treated his brother almost as badly as he had treated me. Then I overheard some people talking about Glavin in a pub when I first got back and they just happened to talk about the old gamekeeper who had been let go with no warning years ago. It was a totally random coincidence, but I started to think they had as much reason to want the old man dead as I had and that might turn the attention of the garda from me. I'm not proud of that, but there wouldn't have been any clues to tie them to the murder. They wouldn't have gone to jail. If they had, I would have written a letter to the garda from wherever I ended up."

"It would have been a difficult time for them, though. Once someone is accused of a crime like murder, the stigma sticks even after they've been proven innocent. I would think you would have a little more sympathy for men who had been treated as badly by Harvey Glavin as you had been."

"Okay, I'm sorry about that, but it had to be done and I needed time to get away before they caught on that I was the one who did it. I realized after I was caught leaving the house that day, that I should be more careful, and that just in case that gardener told the man of the house that he had seen me, I had better do what I had come to do soon and leave the area before anyone even knew I had returned. So, I waited until I knew that he would be alone, after his housekeeper and gardener both left on the Friday and I broke in. I wanted to wait until a weekend because I thought that would give me some time before anyone missed him. I told him to sit at his desk and I sat in that chair that I see the garda have taken away for clues that they will not find, and we talked for a while. I told him what I was going to do and then I did it. I left and got ready to go across to Wales. I used to enjoy little family trips there. There are places in the wilds where a man can hide and never be found."

Bridget and Fiona had been caught up in the story and had not moved from where they stood. "Then I started to think about what had happened that night. I thought maybe he had tricked me. I was so weak and so involved in my revenge that I didn't catch on until after I had already left. I realized that by the wording he had used he had basically pointed to something that would show who had killed him. 'Down under' could have referred to my being in Australia, and I'm so used to the term after living there for so long that it didn't register with me. But I see now that it meant the box that was down under the files in that drawer that would have pointed to me. Or maybe it meant both. So instead of escaping the next day, I had to hang around to find out what the garda knew. I tried to get back here to see if I could find what you just found, but I had to consider that his body had been discovered so I didn't dare come back. I knew about the tunnel since that was how I got in to take Elizabeth away, so I waited until you came and I followed you into it."

"Why not just go to Wales as you had planned?" asked Fiona.

"I didn't want to spend the rest of my life, however short it might be, looking over my shoulder. I wanted to get away clean."

"Well, now you have what Harvey was using to give you away, so you can go. Take it."

"And you won't tell anyone about me, right?"

"Look, Mr. Hooper, I think what Harvey did to you and to Elizabeth was horrible. He had been a friend of mine for several years, but I never knew the kind of man he was, and now that I do, I believe he deserved to pay for what he did. I won't go so far as to say he deserved to be murdered, but I also don't feel like turning you in for what I would call justifiable homicide," said Fiona.

"Nice try. Your husband is an attorney, isn't he?" he said weakly. He had lost any of the vigor he had while telling the story and was looking quite pale and feeble. "I did some investigating of my own."

"Mine isn't," said Bridget, "and I think Harvey deserved what he got. In fact I'll go so far as to say that he should have been tried in a court of law so he could be humiliated in front of the people over whom he felt such superiority. That would have been worse for him than a quick death."

"I don't have time to wait for the slow wheels of justice. And you're just saying that because you're afraid that I'm going to silence you. It turns out that once you've killed a man, killing again doesn't seem so difficult." He brandished the letter opener weakly and said, "I don't have long to live, but that means that I don't have long to feel guilty. I don't intend to spend the time I have left in jail. That means that I can't leave you alive to tell my story."

"Mr. Hooper," said Bridget, "you really don't look well. You should sit down and rest."

"Nice try. You two need to go into the tunnel. Since we seem to be the only ones who know about it, no one will find you in there." He picked up the box of letters and motioned toward the tunnel.

"We aren't the only ones who know about it. How do you think we found out about it? Someone told us. Not only that, but she told someone else, too. If we don't go home tonight people will come looking for us."

"I'll be gone by then." Hooper motioned them toward the tunnel and started to wobble on his feet.

"Please, Mr. Hooper," said Bridget. "I'm a nurse and I'm telling you that if you don't sit down soon you will fall down."

"Fine. You two sit down on those chairs. Bring them over near the couch and sit in them facing me. And don't try any funny business. We'll sit for just a moment, but when I get my breath again, I'm going to finish what I came here to do."

Fiona and Bridget did as he told them to do, and as they sat Fiona tried to determine the time. They had left home shortly before noon and traveled here and walked into the woods to find the barn. That may have taken an hour. Then they searched for some time in the dark looking for the entrance to the tunnel. After they got into the house they spent a lot of time looking for a secret compartment and then they took some time to hear the story of how Harvey had sent Hooper to Australia and killed his wife. She hoped that she had spent enough time here for Charles to arrive home and find her gone. She hoped he hadn't had to stay late at work after all. She hoped.

29

Fiona had no way of knowing that Charles had in fact gone home early instead of late, and finding her not at home, and the dogs inside, he changed and went to the stable expecting to find her there. When he saw that not only wasn't she there, but she hadn't been there, he called Bridget, who didn't answer, and then Sarah. "Do you have any idea where Fiona might be? She isn't at home and she doesn't usually go out without leaving a note for me. I tried Bridget and she doesn't answer either."

"Oh, no. Please no."

"What is it? Where do you think she is?"

"Yesterday when we learned about the secret tunnel I made her and Bridget promise not to go there."

"What secret tunnel?"

"She didn't tell you?"

"No."

"We learned from Harvey's housekeeper that there's a secret tunnel going from his barn to the house and Fiona and Bridget wanted to go there and sneak into Harvey's study. They thought they could figure out what he meant by the note he left. I made them promise not to do it, but I would be willing to bet that that's where they are. And if the killer found them there they could be in real danger."

"Call Garda Simms and let him know about this. I'm going to Harvey's to see if they're in the house. Whoever the killer is might have been watching the house."

"I'll meet you there."

"No! It might be dangerous." He hung up the phone and got his car keys from the counter and drove at full throttle to Harvey's house. He cut the usual fifteen minute drive time to ten.

Sarah called Garda Simms. She told him what was going on and he hung up on her as Charles had done. Sarah ran to the garage to get her car and started to drive to Harvey's when she saw Brian walking toward her. "Get in!" she yelled. "We're going to find Fiona and Bridget. I'll explain on the way."

Garda Simms drove with siren and lights to Harvey's house

and arrived just ahead of Charles Walker. Inside the house, Kieran Hooper was fading fast, but the noise and the lights brought him back to life. Bridget and Fiona also heard the siren and saw the lights filling the room. Kieran jumped up from the sofa, but the exertion was too much for him and he fell forward with the letter opener still in his hand and caught Fiona's arm, slicing through the sleeve of the sweat-shirt she was wearing. He landed unconscious on the floor as blood flowed from her arm. Perhaps it was the heavy fabric that saved her life, or perhaps it was Bridget's prompt attention to her wound. For whatever the reason she was still breathing and pumping blood when the garda broke into the study to take Kieran Hooper into custody.

Charles followed soon after and rushed to Fiona's side, holding her close to him while Bridget staunched the bleeding. An ambulance was called for but Charles couldn't wait for that. He picked up his wife and carried her toward his car as Sarah and Brian ran from hers. "I'll drive!" yelled Brian as Charles sat in the back seat still cradling Fiona in his arms. They passed the ambulance as they turned into the Graent clinic and stopped short in front of the automatic doors. Brian ran for help and after Charles lay her limp body on the gurney, Fiona was taken from him and wheeled into the hospital.

Charles and Brian followed her as far as they could, but when she was taken beyond the emergency room doors they were told to stay put, and that someone would let them know how she was doing as soon as there was anything to report. Charles was distraught. "If she doesn't pull through I won't be able to live without her. She is everything to me."

"Let's sit," said Brian as he led Charles toward a bench. "You need to save your energy. I have an idea this is going to be a long night."

30

Fiona awoke the next morning feeling as if her hand were in a vice. When she looked down at it she realized that the vice was Charles who had kept a tight grip on her hand all night as she slept. "You're cutting off the circulation in my hand," she said weakly.

"I'm sorry," he said not immediately understanding the implication of what he was hearing. When he woke enough to realize that it meant that she too was finally awake he jumped from his chair and hugged her hard. "I was afraid I had lost you and I was wondering how I would ever live without you. And then they brought you back here after surgery and said you would be fine. You lost so much blood. He nicked an artery. If it hadn't been for Bridget, well, thank goodness for Bridget."

"Is she alright?"

"Yes. She wasn't injured."

"What about Kieran Hooper? Is he okay?"

"What do you care about him? He tried to kill you."

"It was an accident. I don't believe for a minute that he would have done anything to us. He only wanted to get even with Harvey. He killed Elizabeth, you know."

"Kieran Hooper did?"

"No. Harvey. He admitted it to Kieran. He said she was having an affair with the gamekeeper. Didn't Bridget tell you what happened?"

"No. She's been with Hooper since she found out you were going to be okay."

"He's dying of cancer. He was on the verge of collapse. If he hadn't seen the lights and heard the sirens he would have been unconscious in a matter of seconds. He cut me when he reacted to them and fell. He's not a killer, Charles. I mean, he killed Harvey, but he wouldn't have harmed us, I know. Let me ask you something. When you found me and you thought Kieran had stabbed me on purpose, what was your first reaction?"

"My first reaction was that I had to get you here."

"And your second?"

"My second reaction was that I wanted to kill that man."

"He didn't have the same first reaction that you had because he wasn't able to be there to help Elizabeth. But he did have the second reaction. He wanted to kill Harvey for what he did to him and more importantly for what he did to Elizabeth. Kieran wanted to kill Harvey for taking her from him just as you wanted to kill him for possibly taking me from you. I would think that you of all people could find it in your heart to forgive him. Bridget understands and that's why she's with him and not with me."

Just then the door opened and Bridget walked in and gave her friend a kiss on the forehead. "Glad you could make it," she said. Brian followed close behind her.

"How's Kieran?"

"Let's just say that he completed the one thing he wanted to do just in time. I don't think he'll last the day."

Epilogue

Three Sundays after the excitement at Harvey Glavin's house, the riding club was ready and able to carry out the last of the dying man's wishes. Harvey had been a horrible person, but no one was ready to tempt fate by denying his final request. So the riders met at Braunleaven since Sarah lived closest to Harvey's house and after toasting the ride and the host they set off with Charles in the lead carrying Harvey's ashes and Brian and Shane riding alongside.

The four women were riding together for the first time in weeks. Anna and Shane had returned after all of the excitement had died down. They missed Harvey's murder, the investigation that put Fiona and Bridget in danger, the trip to the hospital in the middle of the night that sent Fiona to surgery, and Bridget learning about how much she missed the work she had done as a nurse. Her experience helping to save Fiona and working with the dying Kieran Hooper, had made her realize that she wanted to go back to doing something that made a difference in people's lives. Sarah had finally forgiven the two of them for scaring her to death, and Fiona was at last well enough to go back to normal activities. She had been over-tired for a couple of days and there was still pain in her arm where she was going to have what Charles referred to as a really sexy scar.

All of these things were discussed as they rode. On a related note, Fiona said, "Charles and I had a visit yesterday from Andrew Glavin."

"What did he have to say, other than we could go onto his property long enough to spread his brother's ashes on a cemetery that he's probably going to dig up soon?" asked Sarah.

"Don't be so hard on the guy. He's a victim of Harvey's selfishness, too. He had to leave everything he knew and learn a totally new way of life, and he's come out of all of that relatively unscathed. He could have become a bitter man, but he actually seems to be really nice. He brought us a painting that had been hanging in the study of Harvey's house for generations. It's a small rectangular picture. It's a hunt scene and it's called 'The Sunday Ride'."

"Seriously?"

"Yes. He said that since Harvey had wanted Charles to have the desk and Charles had told him we have no room for it that the painting might be a reasonable substitution. Charles told him that Harvey said that about the desk just to leave a clue, but he insisted that we take the painting anyway. It really is quite beautiful. I didn't recognize the name of the painter, but Charles did. He thinks it's quite valuable. Anyway, Andrew said that he and Garda Simms had discussed the allegation that Harvey had killed his wife and that he had done it because she was having an affair, but he told him that he had talked to the gamekeeper and he had said that he was not having an affair with 'that poor little thing' as he called her. He had encountered her as she was taking a walk one day. She had sat down on a tree stump and had started to cry. He went to see what was wrong and she told him about her life with Harvey. The two of them met several more times, but not for an affair. He was going to help her run away. He had talked to the men who had taken Kieran off in the truck about what they had done with him and they told him the whole story. He was going to get her on a ship to Australia to look for him. He imagines that when she learned that he had been taken away, too, that she must have felt so alone."

"That is so sad. That poor woman had her whole life stolen from her and so did those three men. I feel like maybe instead of spreading Harvey's ashes in the cemetery, we should spread them on a muck pile." The other three agreed with Anna on that point.

"Anyway, Andrew has had an auctioneering company take out and catalog the contents for sale and he is planning to raze the house. In fact they will be working on it today when we get there. Then he's selling the front acreage in building lots for high-end homes. He's keeping the barn and building a new house using the back entrance and he's going to stay here. I told him that he could have Harvey's horse back and he could join us in the rides. He didn't seem too keen on it, but I think Charles has convinced him that just because he does what Harvey used to do doesn't make him anything like him. He's really nice, Sarah. Maybe we should introduce you to him."

Anna and Bridget fairly hooted over the prospect, but Sarah was less enthusiastic. Fiona continued, "I told him about how Susan

Phipps and Kenneth Higgins wouldn't have much chance at their ages to find new jobs, and he's going to give them an income for life. And he's making restitution to the gamekeeper as well. So he's not just handsome; he's a good person, too. Maybe that will change Sarah's mind." That was greeted by more hoots of laughter and Sarah laughed as well.

"I think he's a bit old for me, don't you?"

"He really isn't. Harvey was younger than Henry, did you know that?"

"That's not possible. He looked like an old man."

"He didn't take care of himself the way Henry did, but he was actually four years younger and Andrew was ten years younger than Harvey. So he's fourteen years younger than Henry. So let's do some math. He's only ten years older than you. Among adults a ten year age difference just doesn't seem like much. And Henry's age didn't seem to matter to you."

"Henry was different. It doesn't matter anyway. I'm not in the market for …"

"For what? A truly decent, and might I add, handsome man to spend time with you? Someone to take you to dinner or to escort you to all of those charity functions you have to attend? Someone to go for a horseback ride or just someone to talk to? You are a wonderful woman and I wouldn't recommend anyone to you but someone really special, and from what I've learned about Andrew and how he's dealt with everything that's been thrown at him, I'd say he's one of the very few men I know who is worthy of you. And you would never have to wonder if he were after your money, because he's going to be a wealthy man in his own right."

"Sarah, you are still a young woman. You're beautiful, and smart and one of the nicest people I know. Why wouldn't you want a good man like Andrew to spend time with you?" asked Bridget.

"I don't know."

"I just had an idea. I'm going to have a dinner party," said Anna. "I'd like all of us and Charles and Shane and Brian, and I'd like to invite Andrew. That way you could have a chance to get to know him in a comfortable setting. What do you think?"

"I don't know. I'll give it some thought."

"That's all I ask."

They arrived at the property now owned by Andrew Glavin

and rode the path that Fiona and Bridget had taken to the barn when they were there last. When they got to the small decorative fence dividing the yard in two, they went around one end and rode to the right where the Glavin family cemetery sat on a knoll overlooking the estate. The lot had received no more attention from Harvey than had the house. The grass was in some places as tall as the grave markers and sections of the ornate wrought-iron fence lay flat on the ground. The riders encircled the graveyard and Charles dismounted with Harvey's ashes. As he strode toward the rickety gate a figure came up the hill and shook hands with Charles. It was Andrew Glavin. "Would you like to do the honors?" asked Charles.

"No. I wouldn't have the same feelings about it as his friends here, but I did think I should be here for it. I have some really mixed emotions about this. I find what he did to me and to so many others to be reprehensible, but he was my brother. We were actually a very close family and Harvey and I were together 24 hours a day when we were young. Even though he was older than I, he took me everywhere and he really seemed to love me. He treated me well, not like some little kid he was forced to look after. Then when our mother was gone my father changed and I think he changed Harvey. I can't help but wonder how things would have been different if she had lived. It's almost as if it wasn't really Harvey's fault he turned out the way he did."

"Well, we can speculate but we'll never know. I think I'll just carry out his wishes in case you're right about that." With that Charles removed the cover of the urn, walked through the tall grass and into the cemetery, and with a wave of his arm spread the ashes around as much as possible. The wind did the rest. He handed the urn to Andrew and said that maybe he could do the last part which was to destroy it.

"I think I'll put it in his study and when the wrecking ball hits the house in a few minutes, whatever is left of him will go down with the only home he ever knew." Andrew looked out over the burial ground around him. "I guess I should have cleared out the long grass here before you spread his ashes. These are the graves of my family members, and even if some of them weren't the nicest of people, they are still part of me. I'll take care of that soon."

Andrew shook Charles' hand again, and tipping his hat to the other riders, walked back toward the house. But the women sitting together on their mounts noticed that as he walked by Sarah's horse, his eyes wandered up and made contact with hers and they thought they saw them exchange a smile. Sarah turned to see her friends watching her and said, "Okay. So exactly when is this dinner party of yours going to happen?"

Made in the USA
Lexington, KY
08 March 2015